GOLD IN THE SUN

Also by

DUSTY
RICHARDS

The Byrnes Family Ranch Series

Texas Blood Feud • *Between Hell and Texas*
Ambush Valley • *Blood on the Verde River*
Brothers in Blood • *A Good Day to Kill*
Arizona Territory • *Pray for the Dead*
Valley of Bones

The Brandiron Series

A Bride for Gil • *The Mustanger and the Lady*
The Texas Badge • *The Cherokee Strip*
Gold in the Sun

The Natural

The Law Series

Servant of the Law • *Rancher's Law*
Lawless Land

GOLD IN THE SUN

DUSTY RICHARDS

GALWAY PRESS

AN IMPRINT OF

OGHMA CREATIVE MEDIA

ISBN: 978-1-63373-222-3

Interior Design by Regina Hankins
Editing by Gil Miller

Galway Press
Oghma Creative Media
Bentonville, Arkansas
www.oghmacreative.com

For Jory

FOREWORD

Many thanks to my publisher, Oghma Creative Media. The Brandiron Series wouldn't be possible without their tireless work. In particular, I want to give a big thanks to head honcho and design guru Casey Cowan; the editing crew of Gil Miller, Prix Gautney, Gordon Bonnet, and George "Clay" Mitchell; the administration team of Venessa Cerasale and Amy Howk who keep the whole thing riding on the rails, and my longtime friends Velda Brotherton and Mike Miller, who convinced me to take a chance with these guys when they were just getting started. It's a gamble that's paid off beyond my wildest dreams.

Frederic Remington said every time he rode a stage they had a wreck. Down in Mexico where there was no other transportation he rode one to go see some secluded place and sure enough it had a wreck on the trip. After that he said he would walk or ride a burro, but took no more stagecoach rides ever again.

Thanks for taking the time to read with me. Feel free to drop me a line anytime at dustyrichards@cox.net. I love hearing from my fans, and I'll always reply.

—Dusty Richards
Springdale, Arkansas
October 1, 2016

GOLD IN THE SUN

ONE

THREE COWBOYS, UNDERNEATH high crowned hats, huddled around a table in the rear of the Silver Slipper Saloon. They shared a bottle of rye whiskey poised half empty in the center of the scarred surface.

The liquor had mellowed Whit Ralston's concern over his personal plight. He was unemployed and down to his last dollar. The day before, he had met Ben Brackett and his partner Murphy Farnese. They were Texas cowboys passing through town and equally low on their luck. As the afternoon wore on, he reflected on his own poor judgment. Three days earlier, he had arrived in the farming community of Florence with a small herd of steers destined for the slaughterhouse. Old man Cringle, his employer, hadn't uttered a word during the entire trip about not needing him after the drive. But when the steers were penned, the rancher had paid him off and calmly stated that he wouldn't need any more help until the spring roundup.

While he sipped on the rye, Whit knew that his first mistake had been not shaking the dust of the desert town right then. But he'd been so upset about Cringle's dismissal that he had headed for the nearest bar to wash the desert out of his throat and silently cuss the rancher who was too cheap to keep him on until spring.

His second mistake was getting in a card game with tinhorns. Maybe the setup hadn't been a crooked game but half his pay was gone before he could get out.

His reflections were broken when the burly Texan Ben leaned over and spoke to him. Whiskey slurred his words. "Ralston, you been thinking about Murphy's and my plan?"

He didn't know what to say. Ben and Murphy were planning to rob the Arizona Territorial Bank across the street. All they wanted him to do was hold the horses. Lord, all he'd ever done in his twenty-four years was punch cows. But he was broke and there were no jobs in this farming town for drovers. Maybe if he hadn't gotten mixed up with that sweet talking dove who'd stole his twenty-dollar gold piece, he wouldn't be in this mess.

"Blanche!" he blurted out.

"Yeah," Ben said dryly. "She's the one who took your money."

Whit looked hard at the Texan. How did he know she'd done that? Then he recalled telling them about that fetching witch and her trickery. Despite his anger toward her felonious ways, he remembered her smooth skin and fiery movements in bed. He grinned to himself. He wouldn't mind another round with that sister. There was nothing in his tally book like being a dumb fool over a passionate woman.

"Listen," Ben said in his ear. "They got the hottest and prettiest *senoritas* in Old Mexico that you ever had. Why, these saloon girls up here are curs beside them. Ain't they, Murphy?"

"Yeah, and they're cheap," Murphy said. "Why, they only charge a dime a night."

"A dime?" Whit blinked his eyes and drew back. Even drunk, he didn't believe that price.

"Hell, everything in Mexico's cheap—" Ben broke off with a coughing attack that forced him to rear back in his chair.

Whit looked anxiously at his new friend. Something was wrong with the big man. He obviously needed to see a doctor.

"It's this damn dust." Murphy slapped him on the back as he downed his rye.

"I'll be better in Mexico," Ben finally rasped. "Hell, it's green down there."

Murphy lowered his voice and leaned over closer to Whit. "There's enough money in that gawdamn bank over there to live out all our lives as rich men in Mexico."

"Are you in with us?" Ben pressed for an answer.

Whit searched their faces. Whiskey had blurred his vision. What could he do? He was damn well broke, with no prospect of work. He settled back in the chair, grinning widely.

"Why in the hell not?"

"Raise your glass!" Ben shouted, holding up his tumbler. "To all them *putas* in ole Mexico!"

"Yeah," Whit agreed and downed his half-glass of rye. He could hardly focus his eyes on Ben pouring the last round out of the bottle.

Mexico, he kept thinking while his head swarmed. A dime a night… all of them girls pretty… enough money to be rich forever. Hell, there had to be millions in that vault across the street. He'd seen dirt farmers going in and out all day depositing tow-sacks full of cash.

"Are you ready to rob that bank?" Ben asked.

Murphy shushed them, but only succeeded in drawing the bartender's attention.

Whit tried to stand and failed. He slapped the table with his palms. "Hell, yes." On his second attempt to get up, he rose on wobbly legs. His head swam but that only reinforced his courage. He was going to Mexico! Ben said it was green down there.

The three men swayed drunkenly up the street to the livery. Ben paid the stable man for the horses' keep. Lightheaded and almost lost, Whit had a problem hoisting his saddle on his cowpony but finally managed to cinch it up.

"You going to be all right?" Ben asked.

He took a deep breath and hiccupped. "Hell, I can hold a whole herd of horses."

"Good, cause when we come out with that money we want to get out of here in a big hurry."

"You can count on me." Whit winked.

They walked back up the street leading their horses.

Murphy asked Ben, "You see any sign of the law?"

"Naw, just farm wagons and a bunch of sod busters in town for supplies."

Whit glanced around as they approached the hitch rail in front of the bank. One eye closed, he didn't see anyone who looked like a threat.

"Stay close," Ben said under his breath. "When we come out, Whit, you give us the reins and mount up fast. Then we'll be riding for the border."

"To Mexico," Whit shouted, and grinned at his two cohorts.

They turned on their heels and disappeared in the grilled door of the bank.

He was trying to study the bank's door when the barrel of a pistol stuck him in the middle of his back. He thought he had just awakened from a bad dream.

"Don't move, you son of a bitch. Just act like nothing's wrong," the voice behind him ordered. "You keep holding these horses. One slip and you're a dead man. "

"Who are you?" Whit asked, dreading the answer.

Fear was fast sobering him as he fought to figure what went wrong.

"The law."

Frozen in place, he watched Ben come out of the doorway with a canvas money bag in one hand and his pistol in the other. The gun muzzle jabbed in Whit's back. He shut his eyes against reality for a moment as Murphy stepped out next. Neither man realized there were over a dozen shotguns and rifles aimed at them.

"Throw down your arms!" the lawman shouted. "We've got you covered."

Struck with fear, Whit watched Ben raise his arms. But Murphy's face grew red with defiance. He dropped his loot. His left hand moved to fan the hammer of his Colt. There was no time to shout a warning.

The volley of rifles and shotguns answered Murphy's threat. The short bowlegged cowboy was slammed by the barrage of bullets. His body hit the bank's door frame, shattering the glass windows that bore the gold lettered sign Arizona Territorial Bank. A thousand sparkling shards showered in to the lobby and on to the boardwalk.

Murphy was dead before his body hit the ground.

Through the cloud of black gun smoke, Whit could see Ben on his knees. Stray bullets had hit him.

Later in his jail cell awaiting trial, Whit listened to the old man mopping the block.

"Yeah, they got that friend of yours with his leg ironed to a bed in the Doc's office over the saddle shop." The grizzled old timer leaned on the mop handle. "He ain't going anywhere. I'd bet he don't live out the week. "

The swamper spit tobacco on the floor and wiped his bristled mouth on the back of his hand. "Of course, he may be the lucky one. Where you're going might be worse than hell."

Whit drew a deep breath. Prison was inevitable for him. The lawyer had taken his horse and saddle as payment to defend him. He had told Whit that the bartender from the Silver Slipper was set to testify that they had talked all afternoon about robbing the bank. Whit shook his head. His life was over.

He lay on the bunk and covered his ears with his pillow. He didn't want to hear any more of the swamper's talk about Ben or the Yuma Hell Hole. As he squeezed his eyes shut, he wished he could relive the past five days over again. They damn sure would have been different.

On his seventh day, before breakfast, he learned the circuit judge had arrived in Florence. Midmorning, his lawyer stood outside his cell with a grim look on his face.

"Ralston, the best advice that I can give you is to throw yourself on the mercy of this court." The man dropped his gaze to the floor. "That might save you a couple of years' hard labor."

"You mean plead guilty?"

"Exactly. "

He just nodded soberly and turned his back. What did it matter? He would probably die in Yuma prison.

The trial was a whirlwind affair that Whit swept aside with indifference. He hardly remembered saying, "Guilty. "

From his bench, the stern-faced judge passed his sentence.

"Being drunk was no excuse. When you fell in the company of those two, you were equally guilty. I hearby sentence you to three years at hard labor in the Arizona Territorial Prison."

Back at the jail, the jailer took his clothing and issued him wide-striped pants and shirt. He missed his boots most of all. Every sharp thorn on the cell floor stuck in his bare soles.

A week later, the prison van arrived for him. It was an open, iron-grilled vehicle, escorted by two tough guards armed with sawed-off shotguns. They callously clamped leg irons and wrist chains on him and then loaded him in the wagon with six other felons.

He took a seat on the board bench and the wagon rolled out of Florence.

"What are you in for?" the hatchet-faced prisoner next to him asked.

"Bank robbing," he said through his teeth.

"My name's Kildee," the man offered.

"Whit." He didn't want to talk to the hard-case.

"If you got enough loot out of the job, you'll be on easy street," Kildee said.

"Huh?" What did the man mean, easy street?

"I can tell you've never been in the pen before."

"Good guess," he said, not interested in conversing further.

The wagon hit a bump and tossed the prisoners around. The movement jarred his spine. A protesting murmur from the men drew a sharp order to shut up from the guards above on the seat.

"See, if you got the money," Kildee said, "a con can buy easy time. Like being someone's stable hand or some old rich dame's gardener on the outside. See what I mean?"

"What if you haven't got a dime?"

Kildy chuckled. "Then you can bust rocks."

Then his fate at Yuma would be busting rocks. He shut his eyes as they swayed back and forth. The penitentiary was called Hell on the Colorado. He felt certain the place would live up to its reputation.

While they rode, he listened to Kildee talking to the prisoner on the other side of him.

"I strangled that bitch till her eyes popped out."

Then Kildee laughed. It was a cackle that sent cold chills up his backbone, despite the midday heat of the sun. He tried to shut his ears to the man's lurid details about how his thumbs pressed into her windpipe until her face turned purple.

"What are you so pale about?" Kildee asked. "Getting sick?"

"Yeah," Whit said, hardly able to hold down the bile rising in his throat.

At Yuma, he quickly learned about prison submission. The law was administered at the slightest provocation with a blacksnake whip that cut men like knives. Sometimes guards used them without a reason, just to show their superiority.

His cellmate was a giant of a man with a tiny brain.

"They call me Crazy Ike," the man bragged as they lay in their bunks the first night. "I'm getting out of here soon."

Whit leaned over the edge of the top rail to learn when the man expected to be released.

"When?"

"Oh just ten or twenty years."

He laid back and stared at the ceiling. The man was crazy. He'd have to watch his step and not provoke him.

Two days later, while they were on water break in the yard, a con explained about Ike.

"Crazy Ike killed four guys in a saloon fight."

"Was it self-defense?"

"Yeah. But he bashed in the town marshal's head when he came to arrest him. He's okay, just don't rile him. "

"Thanks, I'll remember that." He was grateful for the information.

Every day except Sunday there were rocks to bust.

They were brought in by huge wagons. The prisoners smashed them and then loaded the gravel up. There appeared to be no end to the supply.

Hot sparks from the hammer chipped his face. The sun baked his brains, but hour after hour, he kept swinging the hammer. His arms ached, his lungs felt needles of pain from the fine dust, but there was no escape. Bloodhounds on leashes circled the walled yard as a threat to any fool who might consider running away. The place bristled with weapons and the guard towers were equipped with Gatling guns.

"Have you got a pal named Ben?" an inmate seated beside him in the chow hall asked.

He nodded.

"He's dying in the infirmary," the man said under his breath. "His lungs are gone. They say he still has a bullet in them."

"How can I go see him?"

The con looked around, then dropped his gaze to his food as a guard came by slapping his palm with a stick. The turnkey was likely looking for an excuse to club someone.

"You can ask the cellblock captain at roll call," the man said quickly.

Whit nodded. Since his arrival, he had stayed out of the limelight. Cons who drew attention to themselves received beatings and head thumpings as a reward. He had no desire to be conspicuous, grateful his days were slipping by without incident. His ankles were raw from the legirons and chain. Even his brain was dimmed by the work, but at least he was still alive.

On the following Saturday at roll call, he asked the captain for permission to see Ben after Sunday church services.

A hard look swept the officer's face. Finally he asked. "Is he a friend of yours?"

"Yes sir. I've heard he's dying."

The captain nodded as if he had taken the request under advisement. "I'll let you know."

Sunday, as they marched from the hellfire and brimstone church services held in the yard, a guard pulled Whit aside. For a moment, the action shocked him. What had he done wrong?

"Come with me," the staffer said and Whit obeyed.

They marched to the sick and insane wing with iron-grilled windows.

"I ain't going in there," the guard said outside the entrance. "Your pal is in the fifth bed on the right. You don't try nothing, just stand at the foot of the bed and talk to him. Hear me?"

"Yes sir."

"You got a few minutes, that's all."

"Yes." He went past the sentry into the ward. A powerful

stench assailed his nose when he entered the oven hot room. The odor of rotting flesh, urine, and vomit hung heavy in the air.

He shuffled in his legirons down the row. He didn't look at the emaciated patients lying on top of their mattresses. A wild-eyed naked man was chained to the wall in a spot where a bed would normally fit. The stench of his unwashed body closed Whit's throat as he went by.

He stopped at the foot of the fifth bed, almost afraid to look at Ben, who was dressed in a stained gown. The burly Texan was only a skeleton of the man he had once been. He struggled to sit up. The bright crimson splotches on the front of Ben's hospital gown shocked him. Ben had obviously been coughing up blood on himself.

"That you, Whit?" Ben asked with a strained smile.

"It's me, Ben." He wanted to say and do more but there was nothing that he could think of.

"Ralston, I'm sorry we got you in this mess." Ben tried to suppress a cough. But that proved to be too much, so he lay back down. "When you get out, I want you to go to Mexico and hug them *senoritas* for me." Then he coughed and wheezed. One of the other patients moaned loudly.

"I will, Ben," Whit promised, anxious to be out of the room.

"Yeah." Ben's shoulders hunched as he coughed off the side of his bed. "I'm getting out. But you go love all them *putas* for ole Ben."

Whit nodded sharply. "I promise, Ben. Take care."

He had to escape. The moans and the stench were overpowering. There was nothing he could do for Ben.

When he shuffled down the aisle, the naked chained idiot raised up and screamed profanities at him.

Once outside, he fought for a cleansing breath. The hot prison yard seemed like a clear clean mountain top and he filled his lungs with the air.

"Tough place," the guard said, motioning for him to follow.

Ben surely couldn't last long, he mused as he was returned to his cell. The most merciful thing for the Texan would be death.

That night, he woke up to the shrill scream of the hand-cranked siren in the prison tower. The noise was an unmistakable sign that someone had escaped. The guards ran up the hall ordering everyone up and ready to stand for roll call in the cellblock. Panic gripped the whole staff as they raced about.

As the prisoners stood in line to be counted, Whit asked the con from the next cell if he knew who had escaped.

"Big Jim Sloane and his gang."

Whit frowned. How did this prisoner know, when the whole staff was still checking everyone?

"How did they do it?"

"An inside deal." The man checked to be sure there were no guards close enough to hear. "Big Jim took a lot of gold in his last mine office robbery."

"So?" How did that help them escape?

"The Organization got them out for a share of it," the con whispered.

Whit nodded as if he knew what the man meant by The Organization. Who were they? How could they get anyone out of this fortress?

The following week, word came on the prison grapevine that Ben had died. Whit was grateful for Ben's escape. He closed his eyes and wiped his sweaty forehead on his forearm. Ben would finally have peace wherever he was.

Still mindful of the news of Ben's death, Whit twisted his head toward the loud commotion across the yard. Crazy Ike was screaming and swinging the nine-pound hammer over his head. There was a guard on the ground, his head bathed in a pool of his own blood. Crazy Ike had bashed the turnkey's skull in.

Ike was quickly wrestled to the ground by a wedge of guards. But not before the prisoners cheered the madman on. Then a flurry of flailing clubs further subdued his cellmate.

There was nothing he could do. He shook his head and went back to hammering rocks. Crazy Ike would do a long time in the solitary hole. He could only speculate who they would put in the cell with him. Then he raised the sledge and swung again.

TWO

FLIES DRONED INCESSANTLY around Whit's head as he sprawled on the hard upper bunk. Soaked in his own perspiration, he was anxious for the sun to set so the pesky insects would go to roost.

He frowned at the fall of footsteps in the cellblock. He rose up when a key unlocked the door.

"Get in there, Cordova," the guard said as he shoved a small form of a man into the shadowy cell. "Maybe your memory will get better next time you're in the hole."

"*Bastardos.*" He hissed like a snake as the door slammed shut.

Despite the low light, Whit read the hatred written on the weasel-like face of Ratero Cordova. The other prisoners called him the Mexican Bandit. A lifer, Cordova had a reputation for a quick temper and angry displays. Whit dreaded having to share his small cell with someone who had a reputation among the other inmates as a diamondback rattler.

Cordova never offered to speak so Whit drew his legs up on the bunk and lay back down. He could be indifferent too. But he did not sleep well, considering that another madman was only two feet beneath him.

There were no opportunities for Whit to talk with Ratero outside the cell. While they worked in the yard, the guards enforced silence except for low whispering at water breaks. Besides, he wanted nothing to draw attention to himself. But he kept a wary eye on the silent Mexican throughout the day to see if he could determine anything about him.

Why had they put Cordova in the Hole? That was their most severe punishment. Most men, rationed to only two quarts of water a day, didn't live very long in the iron box in the center of the prison yard. The box's inside temperatures during the day must have reached over a hundred and thirty degrees.

Cordova avoided any conversation with him in their cell. As he observed the man, Whit surmised that Cordova was just a tired old man, worn down by the punishment and hard labor. Despite their indifferent silence, Whit considered him less dangerous than his reputation, though he still watched him closely.

A week later, the Captain of the Guard came in the rock yard. A warning murmur went through the workers.

Captain Stevens was a big freckled-faced man. His blue uniform always glistened and the brass buttons were polished like gold. His red mustache was full and the corners twisted. His appearance in the yard at midday was an ill omen. When Whit quickly glanced at Stevens, he knew the man had something on his mind. Red-faced, Captain Stevens looked displeasured as he talked under his breath to one of the guards he had drawn aside.

"Bring that damn Messikin Cordova to my office," Stevens ordered in a loud voice. "I want that lazy dog to know he ain't pulling his share in this place."

Whit was shocked. Ratero was doing as much work as anyone. They'd singled him out for a reason. Like his time in the hole, he had been pulled out again for some sort of punishment. Whit only dared glance for a second as two guards dragged Cordova out of the quarry. Why were they after Cordova?

Did they think the man planned to escape? Ratero wasn't that stupid. Leg-ironed, there was nowhere to go outside the walls of Yuma. Just miles and miles of rough desert terrain without food, water, or even shade. Whit recalled the condition of several escapees brought back and the guards dragging them past every convict for an example. Their skins were black, mouths swollen with blisters, and their brains fired. The idea of attempting to escape was close to suicide. With less than two years left to serve, he didn't intend to risk the consequences of the desert.

When they did not return Cordova to their cell after the evening meal, Whit decided they must have placed his cellmate back in the iron box.

Late in the night, Whit was awakened by the unlocking of his cell door. He heard a grunt and realized the guards had unceremoniously dumped Cordova inside. Wide-awake, Whit waited until they shut the door and their footsteps were gone down the cell block.

He swung his legs over the edge. His legsirons rattled but there was nothing he could do about that as he eased himself to the brick floor. His bare feet found the smooth bricks and he checked the small-barred window to be sure no one was spying on them. Then he bent down to turn over the limp form of Cordova. Only a deep groan escaped the man's lips. They had nearly killed the Mexican this time.

He went for his small towel, dipped it in the clay water pot, and went back to work on his cellmate. After he wiped the man's face and mouth as best he could in the darkness, one of Cordova's hands caught Whit's wrist in an iron clamp.

"Why do you do this *gringo*?" Cordova asked in a voice more rasp than real.

"I can't stand to see anyone suffer," he said as the man released his arm. "What in the hell did you do to Captain Stevens?"

"*Oro*," Ratero said.

"What the hell is that?"

"Gold, you stupid *gringo*."

He wasn't going to be insulted by the man. Cordova could just lay on the floor and go to hell. He rose and started to climb back up in his bunk.

"Wait, help me in the bed," Ratero said.

Whit paused and considered the request and the fact without assistance the man might have to stay on the hard bricks all night. With a shake of his head, he turned and took the man's arm to half lift and aid him onto the bunk.

When Whit climbed into the top bunk, his cellmate spoke. "*Gracias*."

"Yeah," he said wryly. Helping that hard case was damn sure going out of his way.

"When do you get out of here?" Ratero asked.

He sighed. "In less than two years." Then wondered if he could survive that long. If the scorching sun didn't kill him, another prisoner might. The place was full of madmen and they went crazy from the pressure like Ike and a dozen more of his kind Whit had seen go berserk in his first year behind bars.

"You listening to me *gringo*?" Ratero demanded in a hiss.

"Yeah, I can hear you."

"Come closer."

Whit rolled on his stomach and leaned over the edge of the bed. "Yes?"

"Good. Do you know where the Peralta Mountains are?"

"I've heard of them." What did Cordova want and why he was so talkative after his long silence?

"There's gold hid there."

"So? It ain't doing you any good."

Cordova coughed deep and cursed under his breath in Spanish.

Had he had insulted the man with his flippant answer? He

regretted his remark. The man was not one to rile and then go to
sleep in the same cell.

"They want a map to this place."

"Why not give it to them?" It seemed a damn sight easier to
him than take all the punishment the guards were dishing out.

"They'd probably kill me when they got it."

"Why are you telling me all this?" Suspicious of his purpose,
Whit decided the man was probably speaking the truth. There
were lots of stories about The Organization getting the loot,
then the felons ended up dead. He remembered the three who
had escaped the first month he came to Yuma. Rumors from
the outside were that they had found their bones and an empty
strongbox south of Tucson.

"If I tell them, they would kill me, but if you found the gold
after you got out, you could send me money for tobacco. Maybe
a few *pesos* to grease a guard's palm for easier duty, huh?"

"I see," Whit said, not anxious to make any promise to him.
He knew bribery was the way, like Kildee had explained while
they were en route. But he didn't want to have the guards find out
that he was helping someone they were on to.

"I don't get out for two years," he said, doubtful the man
would give him a map to some kind of gold and wait so long
for any return.

"Shut up in there!" a guard ordered.

Whit drew a deep breath. He hadn't heard the turnkey in the
cell block. Had he been listening to them? No, or he'd never shut
them up. But their conversation was over for the night. He lay awake
for a long time contemplating the authenticity of Cordova's gold.

The days passed slowly. The small Mexican seemed to
quickly heal from his beating. As the sun further blackened
Whit's skin, his muscles grew harder and the callous in his hands
became tougher.

But the nights were a time of rest and the weasel-faced

Mexican spoon-fed the accounts to him about the gold operation. But as he told his tale, Whit began to believe him and dreams of gold gilded his sleep.

Cordova started with his boyhood growing up as a peon on the Palta Hacienda in Sonora. His real name was Raphael, but he had soon became Ratero, which in Spanish meant rat.

"As a boy I came with the long mule pack trains to work the mill. The patron was afraid that when the Mexican government sold the land beyond the Rio Gila that the *haciendas* would lose their holdings there to the *Norte Americanos*.

"So we came quickly. Captain Gonzales led us. He was a fierce man that even the Apaches feared in Sonora.

"The Peralta family wanted all the gold they could get out before the *Americanos* finished the new survey—" Cordova broke off as the footsteps of an approaching guard echoed in the hall.

Whit lay in silence as the guard checked each door. The man's routine seemed especially slow that night as he went through the cellblock.

Lying on the top bunk, beads of sweat bathing his body, he silently cursed the interruption. The silence was heavy except for an occasional cricket's rapid chirp and the sound of the guard's cough.

Mostly he wondered if they would take Cordova away again before he finished his long, drawn out tale. But they seemed less interested in the wiry Mexican and little by little he told Whit the story.

"The mill was situated on a high mesa that they could defend from the Apaches. One day's ride in the mountains. We ground the ore between two large round stones. A mule was attached to a long pole from the center that made the top rock crush the ore between them. I was just a boy, twelve or so, and each day I rode the mule round and round until he wore a very deep path. I never saw the mine where the men got the ore. But it was very rich.

They chopped many trees to fire the ovens to melt it into gold bars. The Apaches were always around." Cordova broke off as a prisoner down the hall began mumbling aloud.

Whit wiped the perspiration from his face and waited for the Mexican to continue.

A guard shouted for the man to shut up, and silence again reined.

"Ralston," Cordova whispered. "Are you asleep?"

"No, go ahead." Whit leaned over the edge and peered at his cellmate. He could barely make out the man's eyes in the darkness.

"The Apaches began to give us more trouble. They attacked the men at the mine and stole some mules. These mountains were the home of their thunder gods. Those Indians had much power and it would thunder and never rain to show us that this was their place. It would scare me, this dry thunder and I would say, Hail Marys all night."

Whit snorted in disgust. That was dumb. Apaches had no control over thunder and whoever heard of it thundering without rain clouds?

"That's stupid," Whit said with contempt. "I think your whole damn story is a big lie."

Cordova snarled and kicked the mattress beneath Whit. "You are the stupid one *gringo*. Don't bother me to tell you anymore."

Whit scowled in the darkness. Cordova made him feel like a silly boy who knew nothing. If there was any gold, he probably would never learn the story, for he doubted Cordova would ever speak again about his treasure.

THREE

DURING THE NIGHT, there was dry thunder. A clap of static electricity boomed in Whit's nightmare. He woke in a cold sweat before dawn. Had he dreamed it or had it happened outside the prison walls?

The next day, he busted his quota of rocks with the heavy hammer. During water break, he tried to get Cordova to talk to him, but the man ignored his effort. As tiny bits of rock flew up from the hammer and spit in his face, he glanced over to check on Ratero. The man hammered with a steady rhythm, his beady eyes intent on his work.

Whit had never known a day to pass so slowly.

Frustrated and angry with himself, he mused how stupid he had been to rile Cordova up and not get to hear the full story. As much a he hated to admit it to himself, he truly believed the man knew about some sort of treasure in those mountains.

The evening meal of gritty sour beans nearly gagged him. He was impatient to be back in the cell with Cordova.

They finally filed back down the cell blocks. Whit climbed on the top bunk and sat watching Cordova through narrowed eyes. The Mexican knelt and prayed, as he did every night before getting into bed. When the man crossed his heart, Whit swung his chain-bound legs up on his own mattress.

When Cordova was settled below, Whit cleared his throat and spoke softly.

"Ratero, can you hear me?"

But there was only silence as Whit fought his frustration. "I'll listen to the rest of your story. I promise I won't scoff at you again. "

He waited, wondering if his apology was acceptable.

Even if there wasn't any gold, the story made the evenings pass faster.

Below, Cordova cleared his throat and, to Whit's relief, began relating the story as if he'd never been interrupted.

"Our leader Captain Gonzales said we had enough gold. He was very nervous acting. This man was a very tough Apache fighter. But for several days, we had not seen the red devils and I think he knew they planned a big attack. Mules were loaded, we were low on food for the deer, and game was gone. Until we reached the Rio Gila we would have little water. It was too…."

Ratero lapsed into incomprehensible Spanish. Whit made a small sound of frustration, which Cordova couldn't help noticing. Whit suspected the man was still punishing him.

But Cordova resumed his story in English. "Water in the mountains was only in the deep canyons."

Obviously, it had been too risky to fill their water barrels under the threat of the Indians.

"We headed down the west side of the mountain. The canyons are narrow, there were many places for the Apaches to fire arrows from. Captain Gonzales was wounded in the throat when they came at us in an ambush. I remember seeing him fall from his fine Barb stallion. The men helped him back up. But we were confused without our leader and we began to retreat to the north, the wrong way to go home. I saw the mountain where we had worked the ore in the direction of my mother's *casa* in

Sonora. I was too young to have a gun and I remember whipping my mule to go faster. Soon we were in a deep narrow canyon and on the cliff above us there was a *casa* of the ancient ones.

"The older men decided the captain could go no farther and the gold was too heavy to carry out and escape. So they planned to hide it in the cave on the wall. It was very heavy to bear, and during the fighting we had already lost two mules that carried some of the ingots.

"The captain was dying. Half our grown men were lost. It was hard work to haul the treasure up with ropes while some stood guard in the wash below. Some tried to find moisture. They dug and found a little water in the sandy wash. But it was bad.

"The captain died gurgling and we hauled his body up in the cliff dwelling. Sanchez collapsed an adobe wall over him and the gold to hide it until we could return. This was a bad place. I was anxious to get away. But I remember the late afternoon sun shown right in and made everything blood red."

An all too familiar sound brought Cordova's story to an end. The guard was making his way down the hallway, rattling doors and shouting at prisoners to quit talking.

"Oh, hell," Whit silently swore. The turnkey was early.

His footsteps rang like rifle shots as the silence deepened in the cell block.

Intermission was another twenty-four hours of prison palate, labor, salty blinding sweat that burned his eyes, and the solitary time of being among a world of like felons. He was equally constricted by chains and the bitter enforced restrictions of the penal system.

But the following night, Cordova seemed anxious to resume telling his story without any prompting.

"We had no leader. Sanchez was no Captain Gonzales. The Apaches attacked us. An older boy by the name of Pasqual and I ran like rabbits from the smoke of the battle.

We raced down the canyon to save our lives. The cactus stung us. We crawled like snakes and fell off dry waterfalls. My ankle was swollen. I hobbled but we could no longer hear the shots or the screaming. I knew we were headed north," Ratero said, obviously upset by the memory of their flight in the night.

"We were lost in the deep canyon, falling down like drunk men, fearing even a hoot owl was an Apache anxious to pound a steel knife in our hearts. We finally fell off a bluff into a deep river. I never saw Pasqual again." Ratero fell silent, there were footsteps in the hall.

Whit frowned, puzzled about parts of the story as he listened for the guard. He was still far up the hall.

"Did you ever go back and look for the gold?" he asked softly.

"Twice. Once with two men. We found the mill but they were afraid of Apaches, so we left. Another time, I turned back because I feared the ones I had rode with would kill me after we found the gold."

"Do any of these men know as much as you do?"

"No, but there is one you should know about…." Cordova trailed off as the guard approached.

Whit half raised in his bunk, wrought with exasperation. Who? Did he mean Pasqual? Was he alive?

He settled on his side for the night, feeling slapped with grim reality. If this Mexican bandit who had slit men's throats while they slept could not get back, how could he ever find the Indian cave? A vision of a war-painted, teeth-barred Apache flashed in his brain. He was having another nightmare.

"Get out here, Ralston," a guard called his name as he unlocked the cell door, allowing a little light from his lamp fall on the cell floor. "Captain Stevens wants you in his office right now!"

Martin was the cranky guard's name. Whit recognized his voice. Half asleep, Whit wondered what was wrong. Had they found out about Cordova's secret? The sun wasn't even up yet. Martin's stick prodded his back as he shuffled along hindered by the chains.

His brows drawn together, Whit worried about his fate. He had broken no rule. This interruption didn't make sense. Inside the captain's office he stood at attention, waiting his fate.

Captain Stevens entered, pulling up his galluses as if he was just dressing, and gave Whit a critical once over.

"It's too damn early for this. But Gruber needs a helper."

"Yes sir," Whit said, holding his puzzlement as best he could.

"If you work your ass off out there, you'll get to stay. That means no legirons, clean civilian clothing, and real food. But if you mess up, it's right back here, understand?"

"Yes sir," Whit said, still uncertain of what the man spoke of.

Captain Stevens twisted his mustache as if considering more. "You better not mess up this chance, Ralston. "

"I won't sir." With nearly half his sentence served, he had no intention of mess it up. Less than seven hundred days and nights to spend in the hell hole on the Colorado. He intended to stay clear of any problems.

When would this trustee job begin? Would he still be able to ask Cordova more questions about the gold? He really knew very little about those places in the mountains.

"Martin!" the captain shouted to the guard in the hall. "Get those legirons off him, have him shaved and a haircut. I don't want the warden asking a lot of questions about this transfer. So he needs to be ready when Gruber gets here."

Whit wondered why the warden didn't need to know, but he was too dazzled to dwell on the matter for long. Evidently he wasn't getting a chance to talk to Cordova again. They were shipping him out to someone called Gruber.

He followed Martin down the hallway to the induction room. When at last free of the bonds from around his ankles, he gratefully rubbed the scarred skin and began to believe all this was really happening.

But he was jerked to reality by Martin's terse order. "Get in that tub and scrub up. The barber's coming in five minutes."

Whit stripped off his threadbare, sweat-stiff clothing, and stepped in the nearly cold water. The temperature didn't matter. He was on his way out.

While he scrubbed with the brush and soap, he wondered what he would be doing and why was he going outside. He had no money to bribe an official. There was something foreboding about all this. He couldn't risk losing his time served. If they thought he would, they were crazy.

At last shaved and his hair clipped short by the grouchy con barber that was brought up by another guard in the middle of the night, he dressed in the civilian clothing Martin issued him. He sat on the bench pulling on fresh socks and studying the new pair of shoes. He shook his head, hardly able to believe his fortune.

"Ralston, you better keep your nose clean out there," Martin said. "Nothing the captain likes better than get a trustee back that messes up,"

"I understand." He didn't want to sound too eager.

"Come on."

He marched after Martin and the gates were opened with amazing swiftness, to his shock. He stood in the pre-dawn light and breathed in the cool morning desert air, practically a free man.

"Gruber's out front waiting."

A small gray-haired elf of a man sat perched on the spring seat of a buckboard. He scowled at Whit's obvious awe and looked impatient to be on his way.

"His name's Ralston, Gruber," Martin said, standing with his arms folded on his chest like he was very important.

"Get in boy," Gruber said, then spoke to Martin. "I'll let the captain know in a week if I want to keep him. "

"Yeah." Martin turned on his heel.

Gruber clucked to the team and they left in a jerk that forced Whit to grab the seat for his balance. He twisted and stared back at the pinkish adobe walls, then closed his eyes as he turned around. It was hard to believe but he was outside.

"Don't think for a minute you're free," the old man said under his breath, obviously reading Whit's thoughts.

"No, but anything is a relief after being in that hell hole." He slapped the knees of the new coarse denim jeans. He had a freedom of sorts. The infernal legirons that had forced his feet to shuffle on the gritty desert floor were off.

"Do you know why they chose you?" Gruber asked as they were nearly thrown from the spring seat by a bump.

Whit turned and studied him, curious about the warning tone of the man's voice. "No, why?"

"Cause you're a short timer. They hate to cheat death and they dislike turning felons like you out among the good folks. Understand?"

"No, not really, but I've got less than two years to serve."

"That's what I mean. If you try to escape, you'll do ten more."

"Well, I'm not that dumb." The wagon swayed and he wished Gruber would slow the team but he wasn't going to criticize the old man and raise his ire.

He paused, wondering about Cordova's gold.

Had the Mexican been planted in his cell so he could learn the story and give The Organization an opportunity to squeeze the location out of him? A cold chill ran up his spine despite the warming sun.

He shook his head as they dropped down the grade and the green irrigated farmland spread before them.

"Whoa," Gruber shouted, pulling his elbows past the seat to halt the sweaty team. "Blow you devils. Well I don't know what good you are to them then. But last year they sent me a boy just like you with less'n a year to go. He finally couldn't stand it and ran off. Course, him and some others had held up a gold shipment and stashed it." Gruber's blue eyes narrowed hard as he continued. "He got ten more years for escaping when they caught him."

"Who got the gold?"

"How should I know?" Gruber acted offended he had asked.

"Well Mister Gruber, I never got a red cent out of that bank robbery, nothing but three years in prison."

Gruber looked him over, shook his head, and clucked to the team. "For your sake, I hope so."

In reflection, Whit considered the gold in the Peralta Mountains, buried in an Indian ruins with the captain's body. Whew, he exhaled. Lucky that he had never asked anyone about those damn mountains or where they were. One word from a snitch might have convinced one of the guards he knew all about Cordova's treasure. Despite the rising heat, he shivered.

"I'm so glad to be out here, guess I'm chilling," he said.

"I know, it works that way," Gruber said unmoved. "You won't for long, it's too damn hot out here."

"What do you do?"

"Carpenter. You ever do any?"

"No sir. But I'm willin' to learn," Whit said, enthused.

"Don't sir me," Gruber grumbled. "I ain't no damn guard. I'm a con like you, only I ain't never getting out. "

"Never?"

"Not with two life sentences," Gruber said and reined the horses to a jog.

"Two?"

"Yeh, I used an ax on my wife and her lover."

"Oh." Whit regretted asking the question.

"If I'd just killed him, guess they'd let me off." Gruber shook his head as he steered the horses around a large chuck hole. "But I wasn't sure who was guilty so I finished the job."

Whit nodded and swallowed hard. He was becoming queasy at the thoughts of an ax murder.

"Hard to explain two naked corpses," Gruber cackled. "Huh, boy?"

"Yes s—I mean yeah."

"What's your name?" Gruber asked.

"Whit. Whit Ralston."

"Whit will do," Gruber decided dryly.

"Fine." Whit turned his head away as they passed a farmer and his wife in a wagon, going in the opposite direction.

"Hell, they can't tell you're a con," Gruber said.

"Oh. "

"No one will ever know that fact if you hold your head up and ain't so dumb to brag about having been in prison. "

"Brag about it?" Whit gave the older man a disbelieving glance.

"Well," Gruber began. "Some do it to show how mean they are and others because they're just stupid. Guess you won't be bragging or telling, huh?"

"No way."

Palm frond shelters. Barking dogs and half-naked children screamed and played in the streets. A few buxom Mexican women looked up from their wash in the brown water of the irrigation ditch.

Whit watched a very pregnant girl still in her teens carrying a basket on her head. The swell of her pooched-out belly strained the material of the short skirt. Her shapely bare legs glistened in the sun. He drew a deep breath and turned to the front, musing how he had better forget about woman.

"Where are we carpentering at?" he asked, deciding that looking at any more women would only upset himself further.

"Up here a ways," Gruber said.

Whit assumed that he would learn all about it soon

enough. To be free of the prison restrictions was sufficient for one day. Besides the old man had unwittingly warned him of something he had suspected—the prison officials might assume he knew Cordova's secret.

FOUR

THE GREAT ORANGE ball was flaming down beyond the
Colorado River. Long shadows reached out as Whit and Gruber
sat resting next to the fresh wooden frame structure that would be
the first floor of the large whorehouse they were building.

Whit silently reflected on his first three days with Gruber.
Their dawn-to-dark toiling was slowly taking shape. The smell
of turpentine still burned his nose and his fingers were crusted
with pinesap. He had learned Gruber was a patient man. But
better than all else, he was grateful to be on the outside without
chains. Even his slightest recall of prison conditions brought on
an involuntary shudder of disgust.

"We ain't doing bad, Whit," Gruber said, bobbing his head
with approval as he toyed with his floppy-brimmed hat. "We
best go get our supper and get back to the shack before some
snooping guard comes by and reports us."

Whit rose stiffly, shaking his head. "This is going to be a
grand whorehouse?"

"You don't need to know any more than that," Gruber
said curtly.

"This is fine," he said, helping the older man to his feet.

Obviously, the project was confidential. The fact that Gruber didn't want to converse about the building's purpose didn't bother him. He was grateful to be working on it.

They were about to head for the back room in Angelo's restaurant where they took meals when a guard rode up.

"Hey, Gruber."

Whit's heart stopped for a moment at the familiar authoritative voice behind them.

"Yes?" Gruber stopped without turning to even look at the rider.

"Make a box tonight, we got us another resident for hell." The man laughed. "They'll pick it up in the morning and take it out in the supply wagon."

Whit recognized the laughter, the guard was Wallace.

"Big or small?" Gruber asked as he finally turned to face Wallace.

Whit remained facing away. He worried his revulsion for the official might endanger his freedom.

"Small, it's your old cell mate, Ralston. Cordova."

"Yes sir." Whit's stomach sank as he considered the news of the Mexican's death. Gone were his chances to ever learn more about the gold.

"So old Ratero died, huh?" Gruber asked.

"He's a dead rat now," Wallace said. Even in the twilight, Whit could feel the man's hard eyes were on him and not Gruber, as if Wallace expected him to blurt out something about the gold.

"Oh yeah, don't use these good boards," Wallace said, "get some cheap ones and charge them to the prison. "

Wallace reined his horse around with a dull clunk of the bits on the animal's molars.

"I know," Gruber said impatiently. "I can handle it."

"Is the kid any account?" Wallace pulled the horse up as if he wasn't finished.

"He'll do," Gruber said without any enthusiasm.

"Well, he ain't run off yet, has he?"

The guard's sarcasm sounded like a threat to Whit, who was glad when Wallace booted his horse in the ribs and headed towards the lights of Yuma. His retreating silhouette gradually blended in with the shadows.

"Sounds to me like they expected you to jackrabbit right out of here," Gruber said as headed for the cafe.

Was Gruber warning him about something?

"You never told me you and that bandit were cellmates," Gruber said.

Whit frowned and looked ahead up the dark alley.

Gruber's probing made him edgy. Finally he answered the man. "I never took my eye off him."

"Yeah, being in a cell with a killer like that would make a man edgy. There was a lot of talk Cordova had some gold stashed away somewhere."

Whit did not comment on the old man's speculation.

Was Gruber in with The Organization? Had the old man been asking about Cordova to learn something about the gold? He wasn't confident he could trust anyone, not even Gruber.

"We'll eat, get us a light from the shack and then go back and build that damn coffin," Gruber said abruptly. "Why in hell's name they couldn't just wrap that damn greaser in a blanket is beyond me. He ain't worth a pine box."

Gruber was upset, but whether it was because of Whit's silence concerning Cordova or because he had to make a coffin, he didn't know. Wordlessly, they walked up the alley and knocked on the back door of the cafe.

"Come in, *hombres*," the boy Benito said as he held the door open for them.

They took their places on old canebottomed chairs at the small table in the corner.

Benito, with his habitual smile, delivered two heaping plates and a stack of tortillas. Under the candle's flame, Whit admired the steaming chunks of meat and pinto beans in thick gravy. Silently, they used the tortillas to scoop up the spicy dish.

Whit thanked Benito when he brought them each a beer. The drafts were never cold, but each evening Whit looked forward to his glass. It was one more privilege the trustee job provided. He savored the beer slowly and studied Gruber.

"That damn coffin-making irritates me!" Gruber snarled, looking directly at him.

"Aw, it won't take us long to build it."

"Do you figure that old bandit was worth fifty cents of boards and nails?" Gruber swept his plate with a tortilla. "Well, I damn sure don't think so. "

"I'll go get the light from the shack."

"No way! You run off and they'd hang my butt for sure. No, I'll go too." Gruber finished his beer. "I can't take the chance."

"I understand, I just offered." Whit looked around the room at the peppers and onions hanging on the wall.

"I know but if you ran off and I didn't report it instantly, I might have to do your hard time."

Whit stood to stretch and idly scratched his neck. "Don't worry. I'm not about to try to escape."

"Fine. Come on, we'll go get that lamp," Gruber grumbled and continued his tirade about having to make the coffin.

Whit's thoughts returned to Cordova's treasure. He certainly didn't know enough to just ride up on that cliff dwelling, but he had a few ideas. How many places like it could there be in those mountains? Where was Pasqual? Had he tried to go back? A hundred questions flooded his mind as he and Gruber hiked back to the shack. He shook his head to try and visualize the gold bars, stacked like cordwood to the ceiling.

When they started back with the candleholder reflector lamp, Gruber broke into his thoughts.

"Are you feeling okay?"

"Yeah."

"You ain't sad about this greaser's death are you?"

"Hell no, at least if I go back I won't have to room with him."

Gruber cackled and agreed. The man's laughter put him on edge.

At the building site, Whit sawed the boards by the flickering lamp. Who had killed Cordova? The bandit had been far too healthy to succumb to just any disease, and he felt certain that the man's demise hadn't been accidental.

The coffin completed, they trudged back to the shack and bone weary, dropped in their beds. It wasn't long before Gruber was snoring. Sleep escaped Whit as he wondered more about Cordova's death and the gold.

A week passed without an incident. Then early one morning a large freight wagon arrived loaded with glass for the house. The teamster, Gruber, and Whit carefully unloaded the windows. They were packed in heavy wooden crates and padded by soft paper wrappings. Moving them from the wagon to the parlor area was slow, heavy work.

"So this is going to be Miss Ruby's new cat house?" the tobacco-spitting teamster asked, inspecting the construction as he and Gruber wrestled with another crate. He spat on the fresh lumber floor without conscience, drawing a frown from Gruber.

"We don't know," Gruber grunted under the load. "Set it down easy or you can buy the broken ones."

"Yeah, yeah," the teamster agreed. "Well, it's going to be a damn fine place when you get it done." He spat again. A dark brown streak slipped down a fresh stud and Gruber made a fist behind the man's back.

"My name's Trellis, if you ever need anything hauled, just ask for me." The man wiped his mouth on his sleeve.

"Sure," Gruber mumbled after him.

The man had earned Gruber's wrath. The old man wouldn't ask for the spitter again if his life depended on it.

Each workday started when the sun shone behind the peaks of the low hills to the east, and ended when it sank in crimson splendor across the Colorado in California. They toiled seven days a week. Material appeared shortly after Gruber sent a note off via some round-eyed Mexican kid. Any contact the two men made with the public was accidental, except for the fat *senoritas* and Benito at the cafe. It was almost as if Gruber and he were lepers.

In the evening, the tinkling pianos, the laughter of saloon girls, and drunken shouting came from a few blocks away. Occasionally, the night was shattered by gunfire from either a happy celebrant or typical fight that erupted over cards or some woman. All that seemed far away he thought of his life as dream-like rather than reality. As he lay on his back, he wished he could somehow shut out the sounds like he could close out the light with his eyelids.

Two weeks passed and Whit's muscles hardened to the new chores. His knowledge of carpentry increased. He wore a floppy-brimmed straw sombrero to shade his face from the blistering sun. But despite the long hours and hard work, he felt fortunate to be with Gruber.

In the early morning hours, they were lathing the roof high above the second floor. Gruber wiped his perspiring face on his forearm and signaled a break.

"You ever been with a woman?" Gruber asked.

"Sure." He recalled with chagrin the dove who had stolen his twenty-dollar gold piece.

Gruber turned back to nailing, the sound of his hammer ringing across the town. "A woman can do things to a man," he said softly. "Like get him to run off, maybe even kill his best friend."

Whit listened as he pulled out a bent nail and pouched it to straighten later. Gruber had a purpose for this conversation and he wanted to learn what the man's message was for him.

"Some women are like that," he said.

"The only kind who love convicts are," Gruber said, looking up toward the peak of the rafters as if he were speculating on the boards they would need.

"I'll remember that," Whit said, watching a freight wagon and two Mexican children riding a lazy burro pass by in the street. What kind of a woman would he meet doing this kind of work? It sure wouldn't be a nice girl from a good family. The God fearing folks knew this was going to be a temple of sin and the others stayed simply because it wasn't open for business yet.

Two evenings later, the pair was nearly home when Gruber began complaining about the heat.

"Too damn hot for me to go to bed," Gruber said as he stopped in the dirt street before their shack. He wiped his face on his sleeve. "You go ahead, I need to sit out here a while and think about my next lumber order. "

"I thought you wrote that down before we left."

"Well, I can change my mind, go on get to bed," Gruber snarled and dropped to the stoop.

Whit shrugged off the man's harshness. The night air had not cooled as usual after sundown. In fact there was not a breath of air stirring as he went inside the dark shack. He undressed and lay down on the bunk. Crickets and night bugs sang their symphony.

The shack was still better than the oven cubicles of the Yuma Prison, he mused, recalling the long sweltering nights in his cell. He was dozing lightly when the door creaked open.

He expected to see the dark form of Gruber come in. He blinked, not daring to move, as a woman tiptoed to his side. Who was she? Where had Gruber gone? His nose quickly filled with her perfume as he watched her lift her dress over her head in the shadowy light. This was a mistake. She was in the wrong place. He sat up to protest, but her palm quickly covered his beard-stubbled mouth.

"Hush," she whispered in his ear with softness of the wind in the pines. "I know who you are Whit Ralston. "

"Who are you?" he whispered.

She slipped on the bed and nudged him to move over.

His breath caught at the realization that she was naked. When she twisted and her bare breasts touched his chest, his heart skipped, and then began to race. He took her in his arms, trembling with anticipation.

"I'm Oleta." She forced her lips against his.

Later, he lay exhausted as she dressed in the darkness. Her lilac perfume lined his nostrils. Drunk from their passion, he savored the memory of her smooth skin under his hard-calloused hands. Finished dressing, she leaned over to lightly kiss him.

"I'll come back," she said. "If you want me?"

"I want you? Oh, yes," he said, feeling desperate she was leaving.

She slipped from his grasp. "Good night, Whit."

He wanted to call out to her, but wasn't sure he should. With a rustle of her dress, she was gone.

In a few moments, Gruber came in. Whit considered asking him about Oleta. But the old man never said a word. He took off his shoes and the rope bed ties squeaked as he lay down. Whit lay on his back and stared at the dark ceiling. Gruber had known she had come to him. Was she bait to learn more about Cordova's treasure? He was still worrying about her purpose when the old man began to snore.

In the gray pre-dawn light, they trudged in silence to Angelo's back door. They took their usual place at the table in the storeroom. The matronly *senoritas* conversed in Spanish out in the kitchen. Benito delivered two heaping plates of meat, beans, and tortillas with his usual broad smile. Both men thanked him and ate in silence. Whit wished the old man would at least talk about his plans for their day's work. But Gruber seemed absorbed with his meal, and Whit decided it was wisest not to mention Oleta's visit.

"Guess when you get out you're going to spend that bank money?" Gruber said sarcastically.

"Bank money?" Whit shook his head. "I may get me a job as a carpenter if I learn enough from you."

"Hell, boy, carpentering pay is chicken feed. You sure can't afford no good life on that."

Was he referring to women like Oleta? Whit was suspicious. "Listen, I ran away from an orphanage to punch cows when I was twelve. I did that for a dozen years until I got laid off my last job. That got me in this damn place. No, I don't figure I'll ever be rich. "

Gruber didn't comment, just put on his floppy hat to signal he was ready to go to work.

While they walked down the alley, Whit wondered if Oleta would ever return. She'd said that she would. A trace of her perfume mingled with the creosote smell of the desert on the morning wind. Dawn cast long shadows through the ribbed framework of the house. If he could get a job carpentering after his release, maybe he could earn a living. His thoughts flitted back to Oleta and he wondered what she looked like in the daylight. He tried to envision her as he cut the sub-siding boards with the handsaw that had hardened the web between his thumb and fore finger.

Gruber was quieter than usual. He seemed engrossed in planning the work as the morning heat increased.

Whit was relieved when a small Mexican boy delivered their usual lunch of rolled tortillas and a couple of day-old *sopapillas* sprinkled with sugar. Seated in the shade to escape the sun's heat, Gruber and Whit leaned their backs against the house.

"How long will this take to build?" Whit asked between bites.

"Nearly your full term," Gruber said.

"How come they don't send more help?"

"Too risky," Gruber said. "The warden might ask a lot of questions."

"He doesn't know about you and me?"

"Don't ask a lot of damn questions," Gruber said, sounding like he regretted telling him anything.

Whit was shocked by his newfound knowledge. How did they cover his absence? This must be more of The Organization's business. Whit felt a chill of fear.

"Besides," Gruber said. "If they send a bunch of cons up here, they'd have to have guards. And they couldn't nail up a board straight. See we don't make no fuss, folks think we did our time."

"Yeah."

"See I like it out here," Gruber said sharply.

He caught the inflection, "out here." The man would do 'most anything to protect his freedom. His newfound knowledge depressed him as he drank from the sweating canvas water bag. There was no way to speak to Gruber about anything.

He couldn't decide what he wanted most, Oleta's soft subtle perfumed presence or the bars of gold in the Peraltas. First the gold, he reasoned. Then they could spend every day in his mansion, between silken covers enjoying the pleasures of each other's bodies. Servants could bring them cool drinks when they called for them. He would never leave the gardens and pool of the courtyard of their secret palace, just savor the honey and softness of her willing body, again and again.

"Are you going to work or daydream?" Gruber asked.

"Work," Whit said, a little shaken by his own dreaming.

The days of summer passed. They roofed the building with wooden shingles until heat drove them down. Then they spent the balance of the day building window frames from the select dry lumber Gruber had painstakingly chosen.

The nights of summer went by with Oleta's infrequent returns. She would come to him after Gruber fell asleep. They were forced to muffle their frolicking lest they wake him. To Whit's relief, she never asked about his money prospects. Once she didn't come for two weeks and he worried that she would never return. Then she came late one night and whispered in his ear with her bare body pressed to his, begging his forgiveness for her absence.

While her face was still a mystery, her voice and touch were familiar. He pondered how she looked when he outlined her features with his fingers in the darkness. He could only imagine the image of her slender nose and full pouting lips. There were plenty of nights between her visits to speculate about her.

A Mexican woman brought them clean clothes on Tuesdays and Fridays, unless they fell on Saint's days, then she came the following day. Their baths were discreetly taken after nightfall in the irrigation ditch behind the shack. They usually bathed on the evening before their laundry came. Shaving was accomplished with Gruber's straight edge before the piece of smoky glass mirror. On the job site, there was an ornate four-holer behind the house that Gruber had built before Whit arrived. At the shack it was always dark and they relieved themselves outside.

Whit soon dismissed his concern about the occasional guard who stopped by and inspected their work with a surly attitude.

"If you two don't show more progress than this, you can go back to the damn prison," were the usual words as the guard turned to leave.

Whit saw the scorn in Gruber's eyes and for the next twenty-four hours he would listen to the old man's scathing remarks about "that ignorant son of a bitch."

In September, the sun weakened. Gruber sent a note to someone requesting jumpers and blankets. When they arrived Whit was grateful, because in the pre-dawn hour when they trudged to Angelo's, the air was definitely cool. The approach of October excited him for that meant he only had a year left to serve.

When the roof was completed, they busied themselves siding the outside, so they could work in the interior over the winter.

During his working hours, Whit observed the passers by. Several times, the warden passed with his wife in their buggy. The man seemed disinterested in the project and Whit was relieved.

One afternoon, four guards brought three escapees by in ragged striped uniforms and heavy chains so the whole population of Yuma could see. The ugly snarling bloodhounds were leashed in the wagon while the escapees were forced to hurry behind or be dragged.

"Anyone ever get away?" he asked Gruber.

"A few, but most go back for ten more." Gruber shook his head and shrugged. "Are you thinking about it?"

"Not me. I told you I was finishing my time."

"Good," Gruber said and gazed off in the distance. "You're making a damn good hand."

"Thanks," Whit said gratefully.

"Oh, yeah," Gruber said, rubbing his hand over his mouth. "We ain't working Sunday. I've got to meet some people and you ain't invited."

"I'll stay at the shack," Whit offered.

"No. I want you to take a lunch and go down on the Colorado River and stay there all day."

Whit considered his words. It was a trick to get him to escape. Damn, they were determined to ruin his chances for release.

"I'm not going anywhere!"

"Have I ever lied to you?"

"No, and now ain't no time to start. I'll stay in the damn stinking outhouse all day," Whit said vehemently. "I've just got a year to go."

"This ain't no trick," Gruber assured him. "There's a place few folks ever go, down on the river. You can swim and rest all day. Just so you're back by dark. "

"I damn sure will be."

"You just do like I say," Gruber said, the impatience rising in his voice.

Whit considered the idea of an entire free day. No nails to drive, no sawing boards, no climbing scaffolds and ladders. He could hardly imagine such a quiet, free situation. If it wasn't a trick, it sure would be a dream come true.

Sunday after breakfast, he parted with Gruber in the alley behind Angelo's. Armed with a lard pail of food and his blanket, he followed the man's directions. Except for a few cur dogs, the whole town seemed asleep.

His stiff prison shoes were a bleak reminder that this might be his last free day if Gruber had lied to him. Near the fishy smelling river, he entered the tall willowy brush. He found the dim path and moved through the forest that was twice his height. The willows opened up to a narrow grassy beach, an arm of water formed by the earthen stick dams used to divert the Colorado's water into the irrigation ditches. He decided this was the place that Gruber had described.

After searching around, he spread out his blanket and laid on his back listening to the river's swishing song and the noisy birds. It was a peaceful place. The sun's warmth found him and he savored a day ahead without work.

Whit heard a voice. His heart stopped and in an instant he was on his feet. Who was coming? Damn Gruber if this was a trap. He was going to kill someone before he did ten more....

It was Oleta.

"Whitney?" she cried and half fell out of the brush.

What was she doing there? He rushed to assist her, his mind filled with a dozen questions.

She dropped in his arms out of breath. "Gruber told me it would be easy to find you."

He was looking down in her face for the first time.

She had a long slender jaw, eyes like violets and a thin nose with a small bump from some past accident. Thick brown hair framed her face. He recognized the pointed upper lip. What should he do?

"What's wrong?" she asked. "Aren't you glad to see me?"

He pushed her away. "You asked Gruber where I was?" His voice was cold and deliberate.

"What's wrong with that?" she demanded in wide-eyed innocence. "I had to know where you were today when I saw you weren't working."

"Does Gruber know about you?"

"Don't be silly." She pulled the ribbons out of her hair. "Who do you think hired me the first night?"

"Where did he get the damned money?"

"How should I know? He only paid me once." She was frowning with her hands on her hips. "I came back because you were nice to me."

"How much did he pay you?" He'd never seen the man with a thin dime. He was confused. Gruber always charged things. She was either lying about the money or he wasn't certain of a damn thing.

"What difference does it make what he paid me?" She turned her back to him in a storm. "Damnit Whitney Ralston! I ain't no lily-white thing and you ain't either or else they put the wrong damn man in jail. You were gentle and strong. Don't go asking things of me. I came back because I loved you."

He twisted her around, kissing her mouth and feeding on the flames it fueled. She was much prettier than he had imagined in the dark. But where had Gruber gotten the money to pay her? The old man had warned him about women. He quickly set aside his concern and drowned in their passion.

Afterwards, they lay spent on the blanket. He could see the churning brown Colorado River when he raised up on his elbows.

"When do you get out?" she asked from beside him.

"Less than a year."

"Then what?"

He glanced over at her bare breasts and wondered why she wanted to know. "I guess find a job carpentering."

"I'm thinking about going to Wickenburg or Gold Town," she said. "You can make a lot more money in my business where they've got gold."

"Do they have a lot at those places?" Whit asked. "Yeah, plenty. They've opened all kinds of mines at Wickenburg, it's booming. And Gold Town is another good place. Men are sifting up pay dirt all around there. "

He considered the two locations. Wickenburg was farthest from the Peraltas. Gold Town was at the base of them. "I guess maybe I ought to go to Wickenburg and see if they need any carpenters."

Her blue eyes never flickered as he studied her closely to see her reaction. If she knew anything about the treasure in the Peraltas, she didn't seem disappointed in his answer. That made him feel a little more at ease in her company.

"Let's go for a swim," he said.

"Naked?" She frowned, looking around as if someone might be around.

"Who gives a damn?"

She shrugged as he helped her to her feet. "Who gives a damn?" She laughed.

Later, they shared his tortilla-wrapped lunch and made love again.

Finally she said, "I have to get back and do some laundry. "

"When will I see you again?" he asked as she rose.

"Oh," she hesitated with a coy smile on her lips. "Whenever I get tired of being away from you."

He pulled on his pants. "Make it soon."

"I will." She finished buttoning up the front of her dress. "This is a kind of a no win deal, ain't it? You and me?"

"I don't think so."

"Well, neither of us have a stake big enough to do anything different."

"Different?" Whit put on the cotton shirt. "What do you mean?"

"Hell, wouldn't you like to see San Francisco? I mean I get so damn tired of this gritty place and the unbathed men here." Oleta was looking far away, beyond the river, past California on the far bank and the distant saw-toothed foothills.

"About like I hated being in prison?" Whit asked.

"I can imagine that." She wrinkled her nose at him. "But if you were free you might not have me."

He walked toward her. "Why not?"

"I charge everyone else."

He caught her by the waist and buried his face in her neck. He hoped she didn't leave Yuma before he got out. No matter, he'd find her later. If he could just tell her about the treasure waiting for him in the Peraltas. No, he wasn't that sure of her loyalty.

After they parted, he sat for a long time speculating on locating Cordova's lost gold. He'd be damn rich. And just eleven more months to wait.

He realized the sun was going down. Wearily, he rose and, shaking the grass out of the blanket, made it into a roll. With the blanket under one arm and the empty lard pail in the other hand, he started back for the shack. He cast a lingering look at the river. It had been a helluva day.

As he approached the shack in the twilight, he could see Gruber seated on a nail keg on the porch.

"Have a nice day?" the old man asked.

"Yeah, thanks."

"I guess that woman found you?"

He nodded, wanting to ask the old man how he had acquired money to pay her. But Gruber rose and started toward Angelo's.

"Come on, I'm starving. I ain't been tasting no damn honey tree all day."

Whit smiled at his back. He suspected Gruber's bad mood was only hiding his good will. He owed the old man for the sweet taste of life that he'd sampled all day.

Eleven months wasn't long.

FIVE

THEN THERE WERE only ten months, nine, and the bitter cold sent sand storms of winter against them. At the shack, they burned scraps in the little cooking stove to keep from freezing to death. Often they wore blankets for warmth, but the chill-laden air still found them.

One morning, Gruber made a discovery on the job site. "Somebody stole six boards last night."

"You're saying someone's taking lumber?" Whit asked as they studied the ground for tracks, but the wind had swept the packed down area around the house.

"I'm sending word for the law to get out here," Gruber said with a hard set to his mouth.

"You reckon we better do that?"

"I hate a damn thief," Gruber growled.

There was no changing the man's mind. So when the small Mexican boy took his note to the law, Whit was apprehensive about the whole thing.

A sleepy-eyed deputy arrived later in the day.

Whit was envious of the lawman's thick sheep-lined leather jacket.

"What do you mean someone's stealing lumber?" the man asked.

"That's what I said." Gruber scowled. "They took six boards off that stack last night."

"Maybe you cons took them and only turned it in as stolen so you didn't get caught." The man seemed grimly satisfied by his own conclusion.

"That's stupid as hell. We only burn scraps. I didn't ask you to come out here to get arrested," Gruber shouted.

"Yeah, well I think. . . . "

Gruber went back to measuring a board as if he had dismissed the lawman. "Never mind, I'll get someone else to check into it."

"Okay," the deputy said. "We'll keep an eye on this place. But it better not be you two doing the stealing."

"Fine," Gruber said.

Neither of them spoke until the surly deputy was well beyond the yard.

"See, we're cons, so naturally we stole it." Gruber shook his head at the man's logic. "I should have said if it's murder or bank robbing you can arrest us."

Whit silently agreed.

At Christmas, someone sent them oranges. Oleta gave them both button-up wool sweaters. Gruber had helped Whit make a small jewelry trunk with carvings on the sides for her. Without money that was all he could do. He wished he could have gotten something fancy for her, but she seemed very impressed and grateful for the gift.

Christmas was a holiday for the pair. They stayed at the shack and burned scraps to drive out the cold.

About noon, someone knocked on the door. Gruber opened it. Three very prim ladies entered with haughty looks on their faces.

"We have some things for you men," the leader said delicately sniffing a lavender scented handkerchief.

Her jaw stuck out just like the rich women Whit recalled came each Christmas to the orphanage. She also spoke like someone scolding a chicken-eating cur dog.

"We think even convicts are entitled to the niceties of Christ's birthday."

"Thank you, ma'am," Gruber said bowing his head.

Whit followed the man's lead and bent over at the waist like a Negro he had once seen.

"At least you are polite," the leader said, handing the basket to Gruber. She looked to the other two ladies as if seeking their approval. Then the three women hurried away as if they might contract a social disease.

Gruber winked at Whit as he closed the door behind them.

"Look here, we got homemade bread, honey, and cookies. Well, bless those old church sisters!"

Excited with their gift, Whit clapped him on the back. "This really is some Christmas!"

January passed and the days grew longer. Light frost on the lumber greeted them and cold north winds brought more chill. Oleta's sweaters helped insulate them, for which Whit was grateful.

The deputy finally apprehended the wood thieves.

Whit was relieved, for he had worried that the losses might reflect on them. The lawman never apologized for his earlier remarks, just said the felons would be dealt with.

After the windows were in place, Whit and Gruber busied themselves manufacturing the door casings. Whit wondered why no one ever came around to examine the construction in progress. But the days passed so routinely that he soon lost his concern.

Oleta came one night, slipping in while Gruber snored across the dark cabin. She climbed in bed fully clothed without first kissing him. Whit realized that something was wrong.

"I'm pregnant," she said, in disgust.

"That's good news," he said elated by her disclosure.

"Are you crazy?" she hissed. "In my business that's bad news."

"Shush, you'll wake Gruber. I think a baby would be fine. "

"Who says it's even yours?" she demanded. "It'll be a bastard."

"So am I. I never knew where I came from. They said Injuns killed my folks but who knows if that was the truth. They told a lot of kids that. After all, how many kids were left alive after Indian raids?"

"Well, you ain't having the damn thing, I am."

"Where are you having it?" Whit wasn't going to be put off by her bad disposition.

Her anger seemed to be dissipating. "When I get too big to work, I'm going to Phoenix, they got a Catholic Mission that I can stay at."

"Where will you and the baby be when I get out?"

"I ain't keeping no damn baby," she said flatly. She struggled to get up and away from him. He held her as his mouth sought the hollow between her neck and shoulder. Shifting his weight, he half lay on her, confident that he could coax her into a better frame of mind.

"Quit it. I'm not in the mood now."

Her words were smothered by his kiss. He read her like a book. Her anger melted into passion and her arms encircled him, pulling him closer.

Although passion ruled his movements, he still worried about the baby within her belly. He planned to change her mind about keeping the child. Even if it wasn't his, he couldn't stand the thoughts of anyone facing the rigors of an orphanage like the one he had. His orphanage experience had been too much like Yuma Prison.

Then he smiled to himself as they both frantically pushed her dress aside, so her warm soft receptive flesh could press against his rock hard, naked body. He was certain that in time he could convince her to keep the baby.

SIX

"WE GOT TO go back to the prison in the morning," Gruber announced as they ate supper in Angelo's storeroom.

Whit blinked his eyes in disbelief. What in hell did the man mean, go back to prison? His appetite gone, he put down his tortilla.

"Is this the end?"

"I ain't sure," Gruber mumbled, not looking up from eating.

He leaned back and studied Gruber.

No doubt the man wasn't talking because he knew they wanted him back inside the damn prison. As his breath raged through his nose, he considered his options. He could slip away while Gruber slept and maybe steal a horse out of someone's pen.

No. They weren't forcing him to run with less than seven months left to serve. If necessary he could even stand the rigors of the rock yard. Maybe they wanted him to try to escape? Sick with dread, he waited impatiently for Gruber to finish eating.

Sleep evaded him that night. The rotating memory of penitentiary life kept him tense. He curled in a ball and tried to summon up the strength needed to survive this final trial. His molars ground tightly together, he vowed to outlive their toughest punishment.

In the morning, after breakfast, they went to the stables. Whit resolved that regardless of what his fate was, he would be able to handle the short time left.

Gruber took the prison-owned team and buckboard from the stables. They harnessed them under the observing eye of the liveryman who occasionally spat a brown stream of tobacco juice in the dust.

"You better have this rig back by morning," the man said flatly.

"What the hell for?" Gruber demanded.

"The Warden," the man spat again. "He's coming back from his trip to Prescott tomorrow and he'll be mad as a wet hen if that's not here for him."

"Let the old drunk be mad," Gruber said hooking up a strap.

The stable operator smiled and shook his head.

Whit moved around the team, checking the harness but keeping his eye on the man.

A large cut of tobacco and spit hit the ground. "Of course, long as he stays drunk, guess them guards can do what they damn well please up there."

Gruber never answered the man. He motioned for Whit to climb in the wagon. "Don't lose no sleep," Gruber said harshly as he climbed in opposite Whit. "I'll have this rig back before dark." Then he clucked to the horses.

A few showers had sprouted the seed of the desert paint box. Yellow flowers carpeted the once barren land. Whit compared the change in the greasewood-studded desert from his first trip to town with the old man. Somehow this time the trip seemed to go even faster than the original hell bent one, even though Gruber kept the team to a steady jog. Neither man spoke.

A guard met them outside the gate. He eyed Whit rather coldly. "Get down, boy." His words stung like the braided cord of a bull whip.

Gruber never even looked in his direction as Whit dismounted. "You can go back," the guard told Gruber curtly.

Whit's heart sank as the old man clucked to the horses. Wordlessly, Gruber drove away. Whit turned as the guard pointed for him to enter the big iron gates. His feet already felt bound with legirons as he walked the last twenty feet to the prison entrance.

An hour later, stripped of his civilian clothes, dressed in prison stripes and his legs locked in iron, Whit sat on the hard bench in the induction room.

He mused how they couldn't get him to run or to disclose what he knew about Cordova. But the prospect of more hard time was a grim reality. They would probably make him sit there until the evening meal, then march him to a cell assignment. He tried to gain comfort by reminding himself how short his remaining term actually was. If he could keep his mind occupied, then his remaining days in prison would slip by. But all that he could think about was the bitter day-by-day hammering at rocks.

A con brought him a meal in late afternoon. The man had shifty eyes and seemed to be concerned that someone might be watching him. He put down the tray without a word and left. The guard stationed outside the door never spoke to the man either as he exited.

Gritty half-spoiled rations tasted flat compared to what Whit had enjoyed at Angelo's. The boiled barley coffee was pathetically weak to compare with the restaurant's. A gray cloud of depression settled on him despite his efforts to fight the feelings.

Night came and no one made an effort to remove him. He took a place on the floor with his back to the wall and folded his arms on his chest to sleep.

From a groggy slumber, Whit found himself being roughly jerked to his feet by two men. The room was still dark. Then a sledgehammer fist to his midsection drove the wind out of him and shocked him to full awareness. His trial had begun. They wanted all he knew about the gold. He was ready for the second blow ad tightened his stomach muscles. Then instinctively, he locked his knees together for protection from a kick to his crotch. His attacker missed his mark by inches.

He struggled against the pair who held his arms. They were both stout men, but all his laboring had given him strength. If he could only tear one arm loose, he intended to punish them. Blind rage roared from his throat as the attacker battered his body with fist after fist.

Finally the one hitting him backed away in the inky darkness, gasping for breath. Whit fought for his own air, still bound between the pair who, vise-like, held his arms. Their fetid breath was in his face.

"Where's Cordova's gold?" the voice demanded.

"What the hell are you talking about?" he managed to gasp.

"This is only part of what you'll get if you don't give us a goddamn answer."

Whit wanted to stall them and try to regain his senses. "How can I? If that damn Mexican had gold what was he doing in here?"

"You son of a bit—"

A flurry of fists pummeled his body. They hurt but he tried to shove pain aside. His muscles absorbed most of the men's blows. They can't hurt me enough, he silently vowed as the beating continued.

Bitter gall rose in his throat and he worried about choking to death as he gagged and vomited. The flush of sour prison food even ran out his nostrils, searing them with the bitterness.

His world went blank.

He awoke later on the cold floor, unsure how long he had been unconscious. Every move sent jolts of pain to his throbbing head. With a great effort, he managed to crawl up and seat himself on the bench. What had he told them? He couldn't remember. He spat the bitterness from his dry mouth.

He thought of Oleta, of her pear-shaped breasts and shapely legs. He encouraged himself, imagining he was making love to her, wallowing atop her naked body. But the pounding at his temples beat his imagination to death.

Martin entered the room. Whit gingerly stood up. "Listen, Ralston if you mention one thing about the work with Gruber when you're in front of the Warden this morning, you're dead."

"Yes, sir." He winced a little as he straightened up.

"You won't get a second chance," Martin warned. "As far as he knows you is just a damn yard bird."

"I understand."

Then Martin ushered him down hall, through a guarded iron grillwork gate and stopped in the hall.

"This is thirty-seven oh nine, Whit Ralston," Martin said to the balding little man with gold wire glasses who sat perched at a high desk.

"He stinks," the secretary complained and wrinkled his nose before turning back to the books. "Take him in. The Warden wants to have all this done by noon."

In the office on Martin's instruction, Whit took a place a few feet back from the great polished desk. The Warden sat in a barrel-back chair and wore a black suit floured with dust. The man did not look up for a long while from a paper in his hands.

When he did, his eyes looked glassy and he squinted. By his actions, Whit surmised the man was drunk.

"So," the Warden began. "Your term is up in October?"

"Yes, sir."

"Well, what will you do then?" The man made a jerking motion with his head as if to gain some sobriety.

"I hope to find work at the mines as a carpenter," Whit responded, "or anything."

He regretted even mentioning the carpenter part. The Warden held a sheet of paper out at arm's length. "Says you're here for bank robbery." There was a pause and he raised his face up to blink his eyes at Whit. "Are you planning any more?"

"No, sir."

"Well, good" the Warden said. "See that you keep it that way." Then the man yelled, "Get the next prisoner in here and have someone bring me some water."

Whit stepped out in the hall. He rubbed his sweaty palms on his pants. The room wasn't that warm, yet his shirt was drenched in sweat. He stepped past a Mexican con who only nodded at him. He moved toward Martin, who motioned for him to hurry. How could he go faster in the damn cutting legirons?

Without a word, Martin put him back in the induction room and left him alone. All this business had him on edge. Would they come back and try to beat him up again? He shook his head—before they didn't want him scarred up for the Warden's interview, that was why they never had hit him in the face. But that was over. What next?

Late afternoon the room became an oven. He napped to pass the time and to forget his aches. He set up sharply at the first rattle of the door. Another guard entered with civilian clothes in his arm.

"Stick your legs out," the man ordered as he took a key from his pocket. Whit strained to hold his legs out level for the man to release them. The irons fell to the floor with a clank.

"Get dressed," the man ordered. "We're going to Yuma in twenty minutes."

"Yes, sir," Whit said, wondering if this was another trick.

In a short while, the same man returned and motioned for him to come out of the cell. He held his breath all the way down the long corridor until they came to the gates. The man gave a brief explanation to the posted guard and the grid iron gates swung open. Outside in the late afternoon shadows, Whit felt a shiver of relief. He was going back to Gruber to build the damn whorehouse. Thank God.

The guard had little to say and it was past sundown when he pulled up in front of the shack and shouted for Gruber.

"What the hell do you want?" Gruber demanded in a sleep-hoarse voice from inside the shack.

"Here's your helper!"

"Hell, he knows the way in by himself, get the damn devil out of here."

The guard seemed to resent the old man's word, but shrugged off any action that he might take as Whit stepped down.

Whit watched the guard drive away then stood for a moment in the doorway. Still in disbelief about his return, he started across the room for his bed, when the man didn't speak up. He almost sat on Oleta who was lying in his cot.

"How in the hell?" he gasped.

Her fingertips silenced him as she pulled him down by the sleeve to lie with her.

"Shush," she whispered.

Whit didn't ask any more questions. For the moment, the whole prison scare was over. He was still sore from the beating, but maybe they would give up asking. He helped her undress.

June, Gruber showed him how to make wheat paste and they hung gold-striped wallpaper. Whit worried the job would be completed before his term was up. The days were long, the sun pushed the mercury above a hundred every day.

The nights never cooled and Oleta's belly swelled.

"Friday, I'm leaving for Phoenix," she said as they lay on his bed together. Body heat rose from their lovemaking and seemed to turn to steam in the confines of the cot.

"Where will you go after the baby is born?" She had no plans to keep the child. His strongest arguments had fallen on deaf ears.

"Wickenburg, Crown King, or Gold Town."

"Would you meet me when I get out?" he asked, feeling almost desperate to keep her.

She shook her head. "And be some sweaty poor worker's wife for the rest of my life, suckling kids and being pregnant all the time in a shack?"

"I might do better than that," he said subdued by her words.

"Better?" she said scornfully. "Hell, we're both losers. No, my maw lived like that. I sold my body to a drummer when I was thirteen. He give me a five-dollar gold piece 'cause I was a virgin. I left town with him. We traveled all over. That old fat bastard told everyone I was his daughter, but he sure gave me a good taste of hotel living and eating. I didn't ever intend to be no one's wife and live in a damn shack like this one. Not unless you've got a lot of money."

He didn't bother to say more as she rose from the bed. In a year, he'd be rich, but she wouldn't wait.

He wished he could tell her about the gold, but something held him back. Their final farewell was at hand. Slowly he closed his eyes. There were less than ninety days left. Good-bye Oleta and she was gone. Tears seeped down his face.

Summer dragged by—painting the house seemed an endless chore. There were chandeliers to hang, and a flock of Mexican seamstresses came to cut and sew the drapes on the living room floor. Chattering in Spanish, they laughed and argued as Gruber shook his head in disapproval.

"It was better when we were alone," he complained to Whit.

Whit wasn't sure. Several of the younger dark-eyed women gave him more than a warm look in passing.

As they adjusted a tight-fitting door jamb, their work was interrupted. A buxom *senorita* with her hands on her hips began to jabber at Gruber.

"What's wrong with her?" Whit asked him.

"Hell, I ain't sure, I better go downstairs and see what has her all mad."

Whit remained to plane on the door while the man went down with his irate worker. He looked up when Gruber came back up the stairs.

"What was the matter?"

"Hell, some of the material was too short. That ain't my fault," Gruber grumbled, as he opened and closed the door to test it. "You're just lucky you don't have a woman."

Whit nodded in agreement. Oleta had probably had the baby by then anyway. Maybe when he was released he could go check on it. A Catholic mission that took in pregnant mothers wouldn't be hard to find in Phoenix. But he couldn't take the baby out until he found work and someone to care for it.

Shorter days marked September. The house was practically finished. As they laid the brick sidewalk in a bed of sand, Whit looked up to admire the wide porch and tall white walls with the drapes in the windows.

"Got some good news," Gruber said, standing up to stretch the stiff muscles in his back with his hands on his hips. Removing his floppy hat, he wiped his forehead on his sleeve. "As soon as we get the yard fence up, you'll get out. "

"How long will that take?" Whit asked, rising to his feet.

"Couple of weeks."

"Couple of weeks?" Whit echoed the man. That would be past his release date.

"They lost the damn papers or something," Gruber said, not looking at him.

That's some kind of a lie, Whit said silently.

On October the seventh, Gruber took him back for his release. Whit had lots of misgivings on the final day. They had little to say to each other on the trip out. When he stepped off the buckboard, he turned back and stopped Gruber from driving away.

"Don't rob no more banks," Gruber said like a father to a son.

"I won't." Whit had to know. "Tell me how you paid for her that first night."

"The woman?" Gruber smiled, checking the horses.

Whit nodded, waiting for his answer.

"I charged it on a piece of paper like everything else." They both laughed as Gruber slapped the team and they parted. Whit watched him for a long time before he went inside the prison office.

SEVEN

IN HIS PRISON made suit, as a free man for the first time, Whit walked the main streets of Yuma while he waited for the stage to Phoenix. He had considered going into Angelo's and eating with the paying customers, but that would be frivolous considering the small amount of release money he had to do him until he found work.

The cheap ticket to Phoenix, riding on top of the coach, cost five dollars, so he ate a tortilla-wrapped meal from a vendor. Wickenburg seemed like the best place to go look for work. According to rumors, there was a building boom there.

The ride on top was torturous and dusty. He was grateful when they came up the brick streets of downtown Phoenix. He climbed down and stood on sea legs for a moment or two before he began quizzing people about a teamster headed for Wickenburg. Finding none, he went a small café and wolfed down a fifteen-cent plate lunch.

Outside on the street, he spotted a double wagon hitch pulled by eight big mules headed west. He ran alongside the off wheel and shouted to the driver.

"Are you going to Wickenburg?"

"Got any money?" the big man at the lines asked.

"How much?" he asked as he jumped out of the way of a rig parked out in the street.

"Either a lot of work or five dollars."

"I'll take the work part," he shouted, still having to run to keep up. "Give me a hand up."

"Where's your gear?" the man asked, pulling him up with his extended hand and still controlling the mules.

"I'm traveling light." He smiled at the man as he took the seat beside him.

"I'm Gil McQueen." The teamster offered his hand by shifting reins to his left one.

"Whit Ralston."

"You look on hard times," Gil said.

"It's going to get better if I can get work in Wickenburg."

"What do you do?"

"Carpenter."

"Are you good?"

"Yes, I think so. I've been apprenticing with a man who was."

"Well, I have a good customer in Wickenburg might could use you if you can really build something."

Whit nodded, anxious to hear more but acting reserved. Maybe the big burly teamster in his forties might have a job for him. That news was nearly as good as being away from the prison system itself.

When they camped that evening, Whit fell in helping the man to unharness the mules, putting on the feed bags, and watering them in the irrigation ditch nearby.

"You're pretty good help," Gil offered as they finished supper. "Where have you been carpentering?"

Whit caught himself before he said Yuma. "New Mexico, but there ain't much going on there now."

"I guess you hocked your tools, huh?"

"Out of money, you do a lot of things ain't smart."

Gil raised up a bottle of whiskey he'd drawn out of the cook box.

"Want a drink?"

"No thanks, Mister."

The big man sat back down. "Gil's fine. You a Mormon?"

"Mormon?" Whit shook his head. "No, me and old man whiskey had some bad bouts, I just don't drink."

Taking a deep draught from the neck of the bottle, Gil wiped his mouth on the back of his hand. "Get my rifle from the front of the wagon and a couple of them blankets for us."

When Whit returned, he handed the man his well-oiled Winchester and a blanket.

"Are you expecting trouble?" he asked.

"A man gets where he can't sleep without a little assurance anymore," Gil said. "They've tried to steal my mules and even rob me before."

"Well, I don't have much for anyone to rob," Whit said. "If you're going to stay in Wickenburg, you need to at least get a Smith and Weston twenty-two. It'll fit in your coat pocket. Ain't much but if you ever need a gun, it will damn sure beat being caught bare-fisted by some thugs."

"I'll do that," Whit agreed, considering the man's advice. He had owned a .45 at the time they held up the Florence bank. He didn't expect to ever need a gun again, but Gil was probably right about some sort of defense. The whole world was gun toting, he mused as he studied the star-spewed sky above. He could remember hearing the shots at night punctuating Yuma when he was at the shack.

Over the next three days, he learned all about the teamster, about his corrals and stables on east Washington Street. How Gil was expanding his freight business to places that the railroad seemed unlikely to serve.

"I'll add a couple more wagons this year," the big man explained as they followed along the nearly dry Hasayampi River's northwestward course. "I've got some old boys who packed for the army that need work. They'd rather pack mules than drive, but they'll work out good."

"Sounds like there's money in freighting."

"Oh, takes such a damn big investment, and then the mine goes out and you've got to find new customers. Just damn hard to get railroads built out here or there wouldn't be any freight hauling at all."

"What about this Marcus guy?" Whit asked.

"Marcus Goldstein, he's a Jew. You don't mind working for one, do you?"

Whit shook his head, amused. "No, I wouldn't even know one if I saw one."

Gil laughed. "Well they're like Scotsmen, pretty stingy with their money. They wear little hats and don't eat pork."

"Sound different," he said, wondering what the man would be like.

Marcus Goldstein looked very young, perhaps in his mid-twenties. He wore gold wire-rimmed glasses, had a swarthy complexion, and a long nose. But his smile was genuine as he extended a hand. Something Whit saw in Marcus's dark eyes assured him that this man was very intent, but honest, maybe too much for his own good.

"Whit here is a carpenter," Gil offered. "He's helped me the past three days and if he works like that for you, well I think he'd make a hand."

"Whit is it?" Marcus asked, then nodded. "Come out back. I have these windows my men made and none of them work. "

He followed the lumberyard owner out through the rear of the office into the yard stacked with fresh-smelling wood. Marcus pointed to the freshly built windows and frames. Whit smiled to himself as he examined them. They were out of square, rather shoddy workmanship compared to Gruber's work.

"Well, what's wrong?" Gil asked, unable to hold his silence any longer.

"They need to be redone. They need to be squared up. A couple pieces of the lumber are too green to be used for this sort of work. You need seasoned stuff for the job."

Marcus bobbed his head in agreement. "Can you work a crew?"

"I'd give it my best. What does it pay?"

"One dollar and a half a day and a bonus after each house if they pass the buyer."

"Sounds like you got work, Whit." Gil smiled and nodded privately as they headed back for the store.

"Do you start at sunup?" Whit asked from behind.

"No. Seven thirty is early enough," Marcus said.

"Do you need an advance?"

"I'll make it a few days," Whit said, shaking both men's hand and anxious to be off. There was a small chance Oleta could be in Wickenburg. He was anxious to check out the saloons and see if he could find her.

"See you here in the morning, sir," he said as he prepared to leave them. "Thanks again Gil."

"Good luck," the man called after him.

Whit waved to indicate that he had heard him. As he went up the street, he was forced to dodge traffic from ox carts, prospector's burro trains, and folks in horse drawn rigs, some even with drivers and surrey tops. Wickenburg looked like a good choice to him. Things seemed to be booming. Six months and he'd have his stake to go search the Peralta Mountains and find Cordova's gold.

As he hurried, he thought how only waiting six months seemed relatively short compared to his prison sentence.

He pushed in the bat wing doors of the first saloon and let his eyes adjust to the shadowy light of the cigar smoke-filled room. He spotted an open place at the bar and went to stand there. He ordered a drink and then turned to observe the men gambling at faro and the card players somberly studying their hands.

The men were miners, dressed in waist overalls and shirts glazed with dust from the tailings. He also studied the derby hatted professional gamblers, with their gartered sleeves and confident smiles—whether they lost or won, they intimidated most men.

The girls wore low cut blouses and swung their hips to bump a few unsuspecting men as they served drinks. Some of them lounged in customers' laps with wild displays of kicking bare legs. And Whit observed that action close. Every once in a while, a girl led one of them out of the room to her crib. This was the way he recalled Dodge City in the last days, except these men were miners, few wore high-crowned Texas bonnets. Cow towns had been good days, but they were gone for the cowboy. He remembered the old rancher at Florence saying, "Won't need no one till fall roundup."

He turned and paid the bartender the dime for his beer. As he started to lift the mug, a tall man in a black leather vest with silver concho buttons and an expensive Stetson hat moved in beside him. Whit didn't miss the fancy Colt with the steer head carved on the white ivory in his holster either.

"Just a beer, Fred," the man said to the barkeep. "You're new here," the man said to Whit though he gazed into the mirror with his cold eyes.

"Were you talking to me?" Whit asked, a little put out with man's surly way of addressing him.

"Damn right I was, con," the man snarled in a stage whisper. "See it's my business to recognize a damn Yuma prison made suit when it comes in my town."

"They sell them to folks," Whit said. "I bought mine. "

"Yeah," the man said, lifting the beer that he hadn't paid for up to his mouth. "If you try anything in this town, you'll be pushing up daisies. What's your name for the record?'

"Whit Ralston. I work for Mr. Goldstein."

The man took another sip of his beer and then wiped his upper lip with a kerchief from his hind pocket. He knifed the cloth back in with his hand and stared hard at Whit.

"Just remember I got your number, con. You do one thing out of line, I'll find an excuse to send you right back. "

"I'll bet you'd like that," Whit said.

"And I hate a smart mouth too." The man exposed his lower teeth as he spoke. "Keep that in mind too."

Whit decided that he had better explain to his new employer about his past. This deputy could cause lots of problems, he realized as he studied the glass of beer.

"That Marshal Williams give you a rough time?" the bartender asked.

When Whit nodded, the man said, "He's only a deputy," just before he moved off to wait on another customer. So what, Whit mused, the man wasn't going to accept his presence in Wickenburg. Whit finished his beer. This Williams would just have to.

He checked out six more saloons, but neither the bartenders nor the working girls that he asked knew of an Oleta. Tired of the smoke and sour smelling bars, he headed for the Palace Hotel to take a room. He entered the lobby and headed for the desk. A balding man wearing a green celluloid visor turned the guest book around for him to register.

"Sign your name and pay a quarter," he said sharply. "Bath at the end of the hall and don't piss out the windows, there's a chamber pot under the bed."

Whit looked up, amused at the man's instruction.

"Well, we have the whole hotel smelling like cooked piss all summer long because guys pee out the window. It hurts our image with important guests." He turned the book around to read it. "Thanks for staying at the Palace, Mister Ralston. Need any help with your luggage? Oh, you don't have any."

Whit took the key and started for the stairs.

The sarcastic man said, "Second floor, turn right."

Whit was anxious for a bath and some sleep. He wanted to be rested for his first day of work.

He pushed up the window to allow some of the heat to escape, grateful he was in the rear and away from the street noise. He turned at the sound of someone behind him.

"Are you lonely, mister?" a woman asked.

"No."

She was older, pot-bellied, her gray streaked hair was mussed up and needed brushing.

"I ain't as bad as I look." She laughed, exposing two missing teeth in the front. "I can satisfy a man."

"Thanks, but not tonight," he said, anxious to close the door.

"Sure, I'm around if you change your mind," she said crestfallen.

After he closed the door, he leaned against it for a moment. Oleta came to his thoughts. Where was she? And where had she left the baby? He stripped out of his clothes and decided to forgo the bath till morning.

Exhausted, he fell across the bed and soon was sound asleep.

The next morning, at the half finished house site, Marcus introduced him to the three workers as their new boss. They nodded and studied him as they lounged around. He waited until Marcus was out of earshot and on his way back to the lumberyard.

"I guess you heard the man," Whit began with his hands behind his back. "We are going to do things a little different. First, I want that stud wall right behind you taken down and redone. It wasn't cut right."

The largest of the three jumped to his feet, face beet red, raging as he came.

"I'll teach you about cut right!" the man bellowed. But his charge only warned Whit to shift his weight and double his right hand. Whit's fist caught him square in the nose. The man was stopped by the blow and staggered backwards. Seated on his butt, the man glanced down at the blood beginning to trickle through his fingers from his smashed nose.

"Are there any more questions?" Whit asked them as they went to their co-worker's aid.

"Yah, we quit."

Whit flexed his sore fingers as he watched them walk away. Not too good of a way to start his first day, he mused. He considered how he would tell Marcus about the men quitting. He might be the one to get fired.

While he considered how he was going to explain, he examined their shoddy workmanship. Gruber wouldn't have lost his temper. Damn, perhaps he should have been easier on the men at the start. No, he couldn't pass on all their poor work.

Full of dread, he headed for the lumberyard. Each step down the twisting dirt lane only seemed harder. Wickenburg might be a boomtown but it sure was different than he had expected.

"What's wrong?" Marcus asked, looking up from his books when Whit found him in the rear of the store.

"Your crew quit." Whit said, waiting for the man's outrage.

"They just quit?"

"Well, I guess I better tell you." He drawled out the entire the whole story.

Marcus listened intently as he described his brief moments as their boss.

"...so I had to hit this one."

"John Tibbs?" Marcus asked.

"I really didn't have their names down that good."

"Well, now you need to go hire some more," Marcus said with a shrug.

"I've been very disappointed in their work, but couldn't seem to find better. So you need to go hire your own crew."

"What do the mines pay?" Whit asked.

"More than I can afford. Why two fifty a day I guess."

"They work twelve-hour shifts, don't they?"

Whit recalled some mines he'd been around in New Mexico. "Sure why?'

"Just let me hire some real carpenters from those mine jobs, we'll work twelve hours a day and you'll have cheaper help than those three."

"Fine."

Whit was already headed for the door. Somewhere in this town's population were some real craftsmen. He intended to hire them before sundown. He had already lost one day's work.

Whit's new crew reported for work at seven o'clock the next morning. Frank Leech, a bearded man over six feet tall with red galluses, Bob Cooke, short and bowlegged, and an ex-prospector who called himself Clay. They followed Whit around the job site agreeing on the mistakes and offering suggestions on how to correct them.

"That's first, then we can finish this little cabin," Whit said as the men scattered around for tools and material.

Marcus arrived at five till eight on Whit's new two-dollar watch. Out of breath, his dark eyes seemed to be searching everywhere as the men hammered and sawed.

"Well, you have them," he said with a wide smile. "And they look like workers to me."

"I'll introduce you to them," Whit said.

"In a minute." Marcus hesitated for a moment. "Deputy Williams was by the office this morning."

Whit nodded. "Guess he told you I did time?"

"He mentioned you were a former convict."

"I did three years for holding horses for a couple of drunk cowboys that intended to hold up a bank." He glanced at the man to see his reaction, but Marcus seemed neither shocked nor moved. "I did my time. Now all I want to do is make a living."

"Sounds reasonable enough," Marcus said slowly. "There is a big opportunity here. If we can build good houses, the market is unlimited with all these mine people wanting to bring their families out here."

Whit felt relieved, Marcus sounded like a man to take this at face value. "One more thing, I can't get any sleep in the noisy hotel. Where is there a good boarding house?"

"Missus Radford's would be a good place," Marcus said. "The food is better than most and she doesn't put up with much nonsense."

"I'll look her up later." He was anxious to get back to work.

"Come by this afternoon. I can see now you'll need more material hauled up here. Besides we need to speak of your raise."

"Raise?"

"If I'm paying these men two fifty the boss will need more. See you later."

For a moment, Whit started to stop him but decided Marcus could meet the men later. As he watched the thin-shouldered man go down the hill, he listened with pleasure for a moment to their hammers and saw sounds. They would not only need more material, they'd need another house to build in two weeks.

The third day, Whit and the white-whiskered older man Clay were building the front step. The past few days, Clay had spoken of his prospecting in various ranges around the territory.

Whit was satisfied the other two were out of earshot, nailing on the roof decking on the rear of the house.

"You ever been to the Peralta Mountains?"

"I sure have," Clay said as the saw tore loose sawdust with each push and pull.

"What are they like?"

"Great stone walls, high mesas, dry streams, and Apaches." Clay straightened up from his sawing. "And damn little color."

"Color?" Whit asked with a frown.

"Gold!" Clay said shaking his head. "I done a lot of panning in them dry stream beds. There ain't much sign of any in those mountains."

"Oh," Whit said, disappointed and trying to hide his interest. Damn lying Cordova, he said there were gold bars from a rich mine. The old man knew all about gold and hadn't found any in those mountains. Whit felt crestfallen.

"Lunch time, slave driver," Frank shouted. Frank had already given the little Mexican boy the pail to rush off and have filled at the saloon with beer to wash down their lunch. The youth's small soles churned dust as he ran with the bucket up over the hill.

No color. The cold meat and bread Mrs. Radford had packed caked in his dry mouth. He sat by himself ignoring the good-humored teasing of the men. Clay's information was a blow to his aspirations about the gold stash.

The next morning he was working upstairs when he spied a familiar horse passing. He looked again as the rider went by beneath him. The bay horse had an unusual patch of white at the head of his black tail. Whit wondered where he had seen such a marked animal before, and then dismissed it, when the thoughts of what he must order crowded the notion away. His job complete, he climbed down and joined Clay who was installing door casings.

"I guess if an experienced man like you never found gold in those Peraltas, a greenhorn at panning wouldn't either?"

"Well." Clay paused and slowly shook his chest long gray beard. "Not so. See gold is where you find it. Just cause I never found any, don't mean there ain't none. I didn't spend a lot of time in those mountains cause I wasn't itching for no arrow in my ass."

"Did you see the Apaches?"

"Damn right we did. A dozen bucks rode right by me and my partner. They never seen us, but we high-tailed it out of there after that."

Whit just nodded and leveled the door jamb.

"Hey, did you ever see what an Apache done to white men?" At Whit's headshake, he continued. "They cut the eyelids off one prospector so he had to watch them torture his partner. Then they stuck cactus spines in his eyeballs. Them mountains ain't got enough gold in them to get me back."

Whit's thoughts seemed to return again and again to where that he had seen that ringtail horse. Then the notion struck him, the animal belonged to a prison guard. He looked around for the small beer runner. When he whistled, the round-eyed boy appeared. Two quarters in his hands and the boy was gone with the pail.

"Lunch time," Frank called. "The boss already sent that boy to get the beer."

"I'll be back," Whit said as he pondered over what the turnkey was doing in Wickenburg.

"These guys are liable to drink all that beer before you get back," Bob warned him as he left them.

The traffic blocked his way and he had to stand on his toes hoping to catch sight of the ringtail horse. Heavy loaded ore wagons became barriers as he checked the hitch rails for sight of the animal. He hurried around a pack train of burros and paused for a man with a buggy, but still he could not find the horse.

Out of breath, he paused and leaned against the stucco wall of Galmer's Mercantile. Up the hill before a small café, he spotted the gelding, hipshot with head hung as if weary from a long ride. He glanced around to be certain he was not being scrutinized by anyone then crossed the street and walked up the steep stone sidewalk.

He dared only one quick look in the small restaurant. Neither man looked his way, before he went on by, flush with the knowledge that the deputy Williams who seemed so tough on cons and Captain Steven's right hand man Martin were talking about something he wished he could hear.

He crossed the street, and then went between the barrel maker and Riggins's Saddlery and Harness shop to come out on Main without being seen by the pair. He would have to be more careful in the future. Martin didn't have on a uniform, so he wasn't in town on official business. What else could Martin and Williams be talking about? He grimaced as he hurried downhill for the house site...The Organization didn't give up easy.

They had completed the house in ten days. Whit left the men with instructions to load up all the tools and extra material in a wagon Marcus had hired. When he came in the front door of the office, Marcus beckoned him back. On the table before the man were building plans, which seemed to excite his boss.

"We're going to build the new mine superintendent's house." Marcus slapped his fist on the plan. "You did it, Whit Ralston. He said there was more craftsmanship in the Wilson house than he had seen in the whole town." Marcus's face was flush with excitement. "Will you have a drink?"

He shook his head. "I don't drink anymore."

"Well, there must be some way to celebrate. Do you know what this means?"

"We get to keep working," he said calmly. His own thoughts were preoccupied with the deputy Williams who seemed to dog his every step. "Oh, there is one thing that I would like and you can take it out of my pay. "

"What's that?" the eager Marcus asked.

"I want a five-shot Smith and Wesson twenty-two and several boxes of shells to go bust empty whiskey bottles on Sundays."

"I'll get you one today. Now look at these plans."

Whit leaned over the table and to study the drawing. Marcus could purchase the handgun without drawing suspicion, for Williams might use Whit's purchase of any weapon as an excuse to cause him trouble.

After the men returned with the dray and unloaded it, Marcus announced that the crew would be starting the next day on the new project and they could have the balance of the day off. The men thanked him and left.

Whit excused himself and hurried to catch up with Clay whose slower steps had left him behind Frank and Bob.

"Well the main man seemed plumb tickled," Clay offered as Whit slowed to walk beside him.

"Oh, he was," Whit said. "Are you going to your place?"

"Figured on it. Too early to go to the bars. All the pretty girls are still a sleeping."

Whit laughed and shook his head at the man.

"Ain't nothing wrong in looking. Gets me in less trouble than when I was younger, you know?"

"You still got your burros?"

"Sure, I've got Jughead, the rest are out in the desert. I just take him and round up the others when I get ready to go."

"Would you show me how to pack a burro this afternoon?" Whit asked.

From under his bushy gray eyebrows, Clay looked hard at Whit. "You're serious about them Peraltas, ain't you?"

"I got my reasons," Whit said, wondering if the old man might get loose-lipped while drinking and spill his secret.

"I don't need to know a thing," Clay said. "Sure I'll show you everything about a burro outfit that I know. Which damn sure ain't much."

Whit considered Cordova's treasure as they headed for Clay's camp at the edge of town. At times he chastised himself for being so set on looking for Cordova's trove when it might only be a myth. Regardless, he was resolved he would go look for it when he had enough money for an outfit and could slip away unnoticed from Wickenburg.

EIGHT

IN THE EARLY Sunday morning cool air, Whit hiked up the dry wash, carrying a burlap sack on his shoulder. The slopes around him were forested with giant-armed saguaros cactus. Obviously alone, he set the sack down with a dull rattle of glass. He had the entire day to shoot the bottles to pieces. Perhaps this would take his mind off the thoughts of the treasure in the Peraltas and Oleta. Her memory had been haunting him, especially at night. She was gone from his life, but not forgotten.

He busied himself placing the whiskey bottles he had collected from the alley behind the saloons on various rocks and along the cut of the wash. His decoration complete, he drew the oily smelling new pistol from his coat pocket and loaded the small rim fire brass cartridges into the cylinder. Pointing at the first brown soldier, he pulled the trigger. The lead ricocheted with a small whine, but the bottle stood unscathed. Disappointed, he emptied the gun. Five shots, one busted bottle. Unloading, he frowned with disapproval as he spilled the mini-casings on the ground.

He reloaded, cocked the hammer back, and aimed. A brown flat pint was blasted into small pieces. Pleased with his newfound accuracy, he aimed again and the next bullet shattered a second one. Then he emptied the pistol. The score—four of five. He began to enjoy his practice with the small caliber revolver.

Late in the sun warmed afternoon, he hiked back to the boarding house. When he started up the porch, the gray haired Mrs. Radford came out the door in her shawl.

"Mister Ralston, I was worried when you didn't come to supper."

"Oh, don't worry about me. I spent the day out in the desert where it was quiet." He paused at the bottom of the stairs. It was obvious the woman wanted to speak to him away from the earshot of the other boarders.

"I just wondered. Do you have a wife that you had to leave behind?" she asked with matronly sincerity.

"No ma'am. I don't guess any woman would have me." He smiled and shook his head at her words.

Mrs. Radford turned her face toward the sunset. She hadn't finished.

"You don't drink or carouse. You seem to be very capable working for Marcus. Everyone speaks of the fine work on the little house that you built." She seemed in no hurry to make her point. "You obviously come from good raising. Where is your family?"

"All dead, I guess."

"Oh, I'm sorry to have pried."

"Don't worry, I got over it a long time ago," Whit assured her.

"Mister Ralston, I came out here this evening to ask if you would join me at church next Sunday. I didn't know your faith but...."

Whit considered her request then nodded. "I would be honored to ma'am."

"Since you aren't married," she said rather quickly. "I would like you meet a young lady that is a good friend of mine. At church of course."

"I'd be obliged." He considered his beard and work clothes. He would certainly have to clean up for the next Sabbath.

Mrs. Radford nodded approvingly and started back in. "I saved a plate of food for you. Come along or it'll be stale."

"Yes, ma'am. "

He was curious about the young lady Mrs. Radford had spoken of. But a nice girl wouldn't have anything to do with an ex-con. Nonetheless, he was anxious to meet a female close to his age and pleasant to talk to. Considering his meager wardrobe, he decided he would have to buy a new suit of clothes.

Monday, while his crew ate lunch, he found the little foreign talking man that Marcus said was a very reasonably priced tailor. In his cloth-smelling shop on Pecos Hill, the man measured and ohed, promising Whit his new clothing by Thursday. After the fitting, he went in the boot shop of Miguel Sanchez, ordered a new pair of cowboy boots, and then chose a Stetson from the shelf at Blankenship's. Hat under his arm, he started back up the side street to the job. Halfway up the steep hill, he spotted the marshal with his hat tilted back, eyeing him from the shade of an adobe wall.

As he went on wetness grew under his arms, despite the cool north wind. His hand sought the small pistol in the side pocket of his denim jumper. He had been so busy with his work and the notion of Mrs. Radford's offer, he had almost disregarded the hard-eyed deputy. Obvious, the man had not forgotten him.

Grim faced, he rejoined the men who were back at work.

"Our boss is taking longer lunch breaks," Bob said.

"Lunch? I thought it was a siesta," Frank chided.

Clay pounded Whit on the shoulder. "They don't know do they?"

"What's that?" Whit asked with a frown.

"Why there ain't no pretty girls go by here, man has to get up on the main streets to see them."

The crew laughed and Whit was forced to grin.

Actually, he was pleased with the progress they had made on the second unit. He hoped Marcus could sell more houses so their work would last.

In late afternoon, the bare-headed, worried looking Marcus came hurrying up the narrow road with a plan under his arm.

"What's wrong?" Whit asked as he took the roll from the out of breath Marcus.

"Oh, I'm perplexed. Some men came by and brought this plan. They asked if we could build it for them."

Whit opened the roll, holding it apart. His heart stopped. It was an exact model of the Yuma whorehouse. He exchanged a questioning glance with Marcus. Who were the men? Should he even ask? He decided not to say a word about its origin.

"I hesitate to do this," Marcus said. "This isn't a hotel."

"It's a whorehouse."

"Yes." Marcus seemed terribly perplexed. "I would rather build houses for people that will live in them."

Whit slowly nodded. "You mean that folks might not want someone who built this to construct their homes?"

"Exactly. We won't build it then."

Marcus looked relieved of a big burden when he started back down the hill. As Whit watched his boss retreat, he wondered who was behind the project. The damn Organization or someone associated with them probably. He would have given a week's pay to know who had come to Marcus about the building. He turned and saw the three men all staring in his direction.

"Get to work, our day ain't over yet." Then he smiled for their sake.

"They don't leave fortunes laying on the ground," Clay said. "A man can spend his whole life looking for riches and pass up the real ones you have to earn."

Obviously his friend did not approve of his search for gold.

But Clay didn't know about Cordova either. Just as well, he decided.

Clay had recommended to Whit that he should use burros when he went to the mountains. Burros could survive where a horse starved. Whit shook his head. There was no way to ride out of Wickenburg on a burro and not be detected as well as followed. He grimaced. Just another problem that he would have to solve.

He glanced back over his shoulder. There had to be a way to leave Wickenburg undetected. He would figure it out.

A cold wet wind swept off the Bradshaw Mountains, frosting the black desert hills with light snow. Whit wore two shirts under his jumper in the pre-dawn to ward off the chill. The men were meeting him at the yard that morning. They were making windows to finish the house. He was busy thinking about the next one that Marcus had contracted when he nearly bumped into a small figure.

"Why don't you—" Gruber blinked his eyes as he raised his head to stare face to face at Whit.

"What are you doing in Wickenburg?" Whit asked, but he instantly knew the answer. He was there to build the whorehouse.

"You're looking all right, kid."

The old man would be tight mouthed about whatever he was doing.

"So you're going to build it?" Whit said, still a little shocked to see him.

Gruber never answered him, just swept on by and went up the hill.

"I'll see you," Whit shouted against the wind. But Gruber never acknowledged a word, just kept pushing on.

NINE

LATE FRIDAY NIGHT, he was nearly ready for bed when Bob and Frank came to get him at the boarding house.

"It's Clay," Bob said. "Tonight, someone worked the old man over in the alley behind the Gold Slipper Saloon. "

"Is he dead?" Whit asked, hurriedly re-dressing.

"We're afraid so. We took him to the Doc's but he's been beat up bad."

"Who in hell's name would want to beat that old man up?" Whit asked, growing angry.

Frank shook his head. "We can't figure it either."

"Did someone get hold of the law? The marshal is asking a lot of questions."

"Which one? Williams?"

"No, the chief, Logan Doane."

Whit nodded. Maybe Doane would learn something. Whit didn't trust Williams.

When they arrived at the doctor's office, they had already covered Clay with a sheet. Whit felt sick at the sight. Clay may have lost his life for helping him. He wasn't certain of anything. He only spoke briefly with the physician to make arrangements for the funeral. In the morning, he planned to go out to Clay's shack and gather up his things. Maybe Clay had heirs that he could write. Downcast and angry over the senseless killing, he parted with the two men and went back to the boarding house.

The next morning, he lingered outside the office waiting for Marcus to arrive for work.

"What's wrong?" Marcus asked as he walked up and produced the keys for the door.

"Someone killed Clay last night."

"Whatever for?" Marcus asked in shock.

"In a frontier town you don't need much reason. I'm going up and close up his things. He may have some heirs."

"Seems strangely cruel. Who could have wanted to hurt him?"

"I can't answer that. We'll get some work done today."

"Never mind that today." Marcus gave a sigh. "I want to go to the funeral. But we do have prospects for four new houses."

"We'll get them built," Whit said and started to leave.

"The funeral?" Marcus asked. "When is it?"

"This afternoon," Whit said, his mind more on the reason for Clay's death than any ceremony.

At the old man's shack, Whit turned Clay's favorite burro loose. The animal wouldn't go far and he felt assured it could survive in the barren desert. Then he circled the rickety residence for any sign of a clue that anyone had been nosing around the place. But the wind had swept any trace from the hard packed ground.

Heavy hearted, he opened the leather hinged door.

A sharp wind whistled through the loose structure. Among the supplies, Whit found a metal box and opened it. There were a few faded letters. He began to read.

Dear Claybourne,

I pray this letter finds you in good health.

I have put flowers on Faye's grave each year as you requested. The cemetery is well kept with the money you have sent and the fund is deposited at the Yarbow Bank. Mister Grey's son is now the chief cashier and handles the matter frugally.

The stone you bought for Faye is beautiful. I know she would have been pleased. I hope in the twenty years since you left Kentucky that you have had a good life in the gold business.

I live with my son and his family in the Wilton Community. He has a nice wife and manages a good farm. It is a shame our spouses did not live to see the joys we have had.

Whit closed the letter as he sat back on the army cot. He would need to gather up the things of value and send Clay's sister the proceeds of his estate. After an extensive search, all he found was a small pouch of gold. He shook his head, disappointed there was not more to send to Clay's relatives.

Then something shiny on the floor caught his glance. A silver concho lay in the dirt just inside the door. Clay never wore such a hammered piece of silver. On his haunches, he studied the button. Why was it on the floor? Had there been more gold in Clay's pouch? As he rose to his feet, Whit worried. There were lots of unanswered questions surrounding Clay's demise.

He turned his collar up against the cold as he stepped outside. The burro had just finished rolling in the dust. He watched him rise and shake the dirt from his coat. Perhaps, Marcus could write the letter to Clay's sister. Whit turned the concho over deep in his pocket. If there had been a thief, he had been very neat to leave everything intact. Perhaps, Whit mused as he hurried back to town, nothing was amiss and he was just being overly suspicious.

When he entered the marshal's office, an older heavyset man with a bushy gray mustache turned from a desk piled with papers.

"What can I do for you?" he asked.

"Whit Ralston." He waited as the big man gave him a critical appraisal.

"Logan Doone," the man offered. "I'm the chief here. "

"Marshal Doone, an employee of the Marcus Construction Company was killed last night. Clay Murchison had a few personal effects that I thought should be sent to his heirs."

He put the small box on the man's desk. The lawman searched through it and returned his gaze to Whit.

"I'd also like to send his sister twenty dollars for his burros and pack gear," Whit said, realizing his true intention would be out when Williams learned the details.

"That sounds fair. My deputy tells me you are an ex-con?"

"I am."

"You seem to be a model citizen." Doone nodded his head in approval. "Your building skills are a great addition to our city. Just wish I could afford one myself. Yes, go ahead and send that box to his people."

"Thanks," Whit said and as he turned he saw a familiar leather vest hanging by the gun rack. Was it missing a concho? There was no way to go over and check without being obvious.

"Oh, bring it by when you get ready to mail it," Doone said and turned back to his papers. "Then I'll know it was done."

"Sure," Whit said, still wondering if the vest was without a silver button. But there was more than that to concern him. Clay's funeral, cashing the gold, and his work—he might need supplies before Monday. He tried to shake the guilt he felt that the old man might have been killed for his involvement with him.

TEN

"WASN'T YOU LOOKING for a saloon gal name of Oleta?" the man in front of the Rio Cafe asked Whit in the predawn. A rough bearded man with hard dark eyes and a shapeless hat. "I seen you last fall when you first come to town. Think it was up in the Pearl Lady, you was asking about her."

"Have you seen her?"

"Two days ago in Gold Town." The man grinned with pride. "About so tall, blue eyes and brown hair."

"Thanks," Whit said, considering the information.

"Yes sir, just figured you needed to know. I fell in love with a saloon gal once," the man said with empathy.

"Sure." Whit pushed on. She was a big girl. She could take care of herself. But why had she gone there? Gold Town was at the northern base of the Peraltas Mountains. Wickenburg or Crown King would have been much richer pickings.

He hurried on. He needed to order material for the men. She was back plying her trade. Where had she left the child? He soon forgot her and busied himself with his job.

Saturday, he decided to move Clay's lead burro Jughead to the stables in town.

"What is so damn special about this jas-honkey?" Liggett, the tall bean pole of a livery operator asked, as he eyed the burro between a spit of juicy brown tobacco.

"He belonged to a friend," Whit said as he watched the burro lay his ears back and charge the horse that threatened his arrival.

"He could just wander around for free like all the others," Liggett protested, referring to all the other loose burros in town.

"I'll pay the bill." He left, smiling at the man's mumbling.

Clay had said this one was special. He could smell Apaches. Whit wanted to believe he could do that and was worth the ten cents a day Leggett charged him. He drew a deep breath. Frank and Bob both had separate crews. There was a lot to check on. He headed uphill to the first site.

As he climbed, the growing skeleton of Gruber's project came into view. He'd heard they had hired him some Mexican helpers and the old man lived in a nearby adobe hovel. Whit was grateful their paths had not crossed again, since the first meeting had been so awkward. What had Gruber said? He would do anything to stay outside the prison walls. There was enough to do not to worry about his former mentor.

Sunday, he accompanied Mrs. Radford to church.

In his new suit and Stetson, he walked with the lady.

"I wonder what Reverend Blanes will speak about this morning?" she asked, making obvious conversation.

"Oh, probably the scriptures."

"Yes."

"I'm not an embarrassment to you am I?" Whit asked.

"Why heaven's no. I don't have a son, but if I did I would hope he did as well as you are doing."

"You see good things in folks."

"No, why just last week Judge Barnes said what a valuable addition you'd become to this community."

"Yes ma'am," he said softly. Judge Barnes was a big man with a gold chain on his impressive pocket watch, aloof and in his late forties. His pleasant wife Helen was always well dressed and their daughter was the blue-eyed girl, hardly out of her teens, whom he had spoken to the first Sunday.

After services were over, he waited patiently for Mrs. Radford to finish visiting with the church ladies in front of the chapel. Helen Barnes came across from the steps.

"Mister Ralston?" the woman asked hesitantly.

"Yes ma'am," he said, a little taken back by her approach.

"The Judge and I would like you to come to our house for dinner at two. If you don't have plans."

"Of course, he will," Mrs. Radford said, as if he was incapable of answering for himself. "He'll probably be glad to escape boarding house food."

"Then we shall see you at two?" Helen asked.

"Yes," he agreed, still taken back by the invitation. But he did notice how the blue-eyed girl demurely looked away when his glance met hers. He also observed the small puff of cigarette smoke in the doorway across the street. The deputy was watching, although he couldn't see him.

"You were going to accept the Barnes invitation, weren't you?" Mrs. Radford asked as they walked back to the boarding house.

"No ma'am. I kinda figured that I didn't belong there. "

"Nonsense," she said in a very determined tone. "You are one of this town's most eligible bachelors."

His face heated up. "I'm just a carpenter."

"Well not for long," she said firmly.

He drew a long deep breath. His boarding house lady had set her cap for his social mixing, like it or not.

He paused at the wrought iron gate. Impressed with the Barnes' white two-story structure, he wondered if he should go to the side door as he considered the fancy inlaid glass front door at the head of the brick walk.

At his hesitant knock, a maid ushered him in and took his hat. The ponderous form of Judge Barnes appeared down the dark hallway with the polished floor.

"Ralston," the man's voice boomed. "Nice of you to come. Join me in the library."

The room was filled with leather bound books. The judge indicated a high back leather chair for him. Then he took a seat opposite Whit.

"Well, you and Marcos seem to be doing a rather good business these days."

"Yes, we're busy," Whit said, wringing his hands before he forced himself to grasp the chair arms so he would not appear overly nervous.

"I know about your past." The judge's tone was matter-of-fact.

"I've been trying to live that down," Whit said softly.

"You've done a good job of it. Tell me, what do you know about this sin palace that's being built?"

"We turned it down," Whit said. "Marcus and I felt it would be bad for our home building business."

"Yes, but who is this contractor?"

"You mean Gruber, the old man? He's a lifer."

The judge shook his head. "I guess he does more good outside than in. No, whose money is behind it?"

"I worked on the one in Yuma and never did know who paid for it."

"Yes, there is another there. Lots of money for a bordello and the owners are so mysterious, wouldn't you say?"

"Yes, sir."

"My friends just call me Judge." He smiled.

"Judge, it will be," Whit said, relieved at the man's openness.

"Then you shall be Whit." The man rose as the maid came to the doorway and announced dinner was ready.

Whit was impressed with the house's interior.

Barnes had made some money, the whole mansion showed plenty of expensive items.

Why the quiz in the library? Whit pondered on the whole conversation as they went to the dining room area. Entering, he caught the eye of the Barnes daughter. She was very attractive, with a smooth, clear complexion, and a straight line of pearly white teeth. Her youthful figure in the starched dress warmed him.

"Mister Ralston, do you take coffee with your meal?" she asked.

"Whit," he said, looking deeply into her blue eyes. "Coffee is fine.'

"Whit," she repeated as if testing the name on her tongue. She seemed immobilized across the great linen-clothed table set with fine china and crystal glassware.

In his mind, the dull gold bars glinted in a pile as he thought of Cordova's treasure. Someday, he would have such a house and a wife like Mary Jo Barnes.

He tried to compare her to the voluptuous Oleta. Imagining both women, he wondered whom he would choose. This very proper straight-backed maiden before him was certainly different than any woman he had known. Mary Jo reminded him of expensive bone china, too fragile and delicate for a man of his past.

The pleasant conversation during the meal dwelled on his business. There were questions about the new homes he had in progress and their owners. Despite the formality of the setting, he felt himself relaxing.

"Mister Ralston... Whit?" Mary Jo asked across the table. "Have you ever tasted Mister Whipple's bubbly sarsaparilla?"

"No, ma'am," he said as if a great barrier had just dissolved between them and this beautiful girl was a longtime acquaintance.

"Would it be a terrible inconvenience for you to escort me there this afternoon for a small cup?"

"No, it certainly won't be." He was certain he wanted to go, but not sure if this was the time. "Do we need to help here?"

"No, you young people run along," the judge assured them.

Whit wasn't sure of anything for he stared at her as they both rose to their feet.

"I am sure Mister Ralston will be good company.

"There are some rather scruffy characters on the streets," Helen said with an approving smile.

"Mother," Mary Jo said looking up as if for assistance. "We are only going to the drug store."

"Yes. Whit, did you get enough to eat before my impulsive daughter drags you off?" her mother asked.

"I'm fine. Thanks for having me."

"Come again," the judge said, checking his great timepiece.

Mary Jo bounced back in the room with an expensive Spanish shawl over her head. "Shall we go to the ball?" she jested.

"Tell the governor hello." The judge laughed.

"Oh, we will." She led Whit off down the hall.

Once on the porch he put on his new hat. She shook her head in disapproval. "You look too solemn. I am not a very sophisticated lady. I really hate at times being the judge's daughter."

"All that you have. Why there are folks that would do anything for all that."

"Our family used to be pirates." Then when she saw the shock in his eyes, she laughed. "No, they were an old new

England Shipping company. My father took an appointment here as a territorial judge. We came west for mother's health."

He was pleased that she lightly held his arm as they started down the walk.

"Do you think I am some fallen… woman, asking you out for sarsaparilla?" she asked, in a subdued tone.

"No," he said quickly to assure her.

"Good. I saved you from being subjected to an afternoon of long speeches on statehood and politics—where I would have had to sit with my hands folded in my lap."

He warmed with her laughter as they walked down the steep, crooked street. He felt as if he were dancing with her in a great ballroom. Light footed, he imagined carrying her around in a waltz through a great courtroom full of royalty. Strange, he mused, the only women he had ever danced with before were saloon girls, and then he had been too inebriated to care.

In the drug store, they sat at one of the small tables. Sipping bubbly sarsaparilla elevated both their moods. He was proud of his semi possession of this beautiful girl. He dreaded when the afternoon would end.

"Now that we have finished our sinful Sabbath pleasure, shall we go for a walk around town?" she asked.

"There isn't really much to see," he said wishing he could think of an excuse to stall her return.

"Is there water in the river?"

"We can go see," he said, grateful for her notion. When he assisted her with the shawl, he noticed the deputy. Lounging in the doorway across the street, Williams's figure was almost obliterated by the inverted gold letters on the drugstore's plate glass. The man's cold stare was unmistakable.

Whit paid the young attendant for their drinks and, with her on his arm, swept out on the shady porch.

"Don't look now," he said under his breath. "There is a deputy marshal across the street that has a deep interest in you and your welfare."

"You must be teasing me."

"I suspect he is guarding you."

"That is crazy. Why that's Deputy Williams." She turned back. "He is just doing his job."

"All right," he said, resolved not to frighten her away, but his conscience forced him to explain to her. "You don't know much about me," he said as they strolled down the boardwalk. "I use to ride with outlaws."

"Were they famous?"

"Mary Jo, I'm being serious with you."

She took a better hold of his arm. "So am I. I don't care about your past. You didn't kill anyone did you?"

"No." He recalled the gunfight in front of the bank. "But do you understand, I'm not the kind of guy nice young ladies go out with."

"I think you were very honest to tell me all this. And I think you are far too serious."

"I don't believe you understand," he protested as they started down the sandy lane that led to the towering leafless cottonwoods and the river.

"Whit Ralston, my father knew all about you before we ever invited you to dinner. Would you think he would let his daughter go off for a drug store drink with a hardened criminal?"

"I guess not." He reflected as they poised on the high bank and watched the silt-laden water swirl and splash past them. He turned and looked into her eyes. Impulsively he swiftly took her in his arms and softly kissed her on the mouth. Then feeling self-conscious, he released her.

"I asked for that," she said coolly.

"My fault, I am way too brash." He studied the dusty toes of his new boots.

"What will happen now?"

"Well—you haven't been violated," he said almost angrily.

She laughed and took his arm. "Silly, you don't understand. If I am that easy to kiss, my next question is will you ever return?"

"Whatever do you mean? Of course, I'll be back until they run out of sarsaparilla."

"That's a big relief." She hooked her arm deeper in his.

Whit was filled with a newfound power in his life. He could not remember ever feeling this good, at least not when he was sober. Mary Jo Barnes was a delightful puzzle.

ELEVEN

THE DESERT COOLNESS swept his face in the pre-dawn darkness that engulfed Wickenburg. Whit stepped off the boarding house porch. Early enough to check his construction site before the crews started work, he stretched his legs as he strode downhill. His mind filled with a dozen items he must have ready for the day ahead, he never saw the assailant.

A sharp pain exploded in his head. His knees struck the stone walk as the attacker hit him again and he sprawled face down, barely conscious.

"Stay away!" The voice was far away and seemed unreal. The toe of the boot that repeatedly struck his ribs made his eyes flash in red pain. There were curse words mixed with the kicking, but he soon lost consciousness.

He opened his eyes and recognized the boarding house room surrounded by concerned faces. Someone bent over him but he only saw a hazy fog of the man's face.

"He's coming around," Marcus said loudly.

He could see them clearer, standing at his bedside—Bob, Frank, Mrs. Rathford, and Mary Jo. Doc Branigan nodded in approval.

"Who did this?" Frank demanded.

"I never saw them...." He lay back to endure the throbbing in his skull. Fighting to regain his words, he shook his head at the revenge-filled look in Frank and Bob's faces. He then realized his ribs were taped. Lifting his arm seemed almost life-threatening because of the pain the movement caused.

"You lie still," the doctor warned. "Do you hear me?"

"Yes. You guys go back to work. I'll find whoever did this."

"If we don't first," Frank said and they left.

Mrs. Radford even hustled the worried Marcus out after them.

"What time is it?" Whit asked.

"Ten a.m.," the boarding house lady said.

"Monday?"

"No, Tuesday," Mrs. Radford said. "Mary Jo is going to sit with you if you promise not to wear yourself out talking to her. I have things to do."

"I promise." He smiled at the fresh face staring down at him. In her starched dress and her hair fixed back she looked like an angel.

"Did you tell the men you didn't know who beat you up so they wouldn't go after the one who did it?" she asked.

"No, I'm not sure," he said as she grasped his calloused hand and sat down on the chair beside the bed.

"You did a lot of talking while you were out."

"Did it make any sense?"

"No, last night you kept calling for Goober." She shook her head. "Then you yelled they'd killed a rat. It was almost funny. You sounded like this rat was something you really liked."

"I must have been crazy," he said, fearful that he might have revealed more.

"How is your patient?" Mrs. Radford asked, bearing a tray with food.

"Talking sensible," Mary Jo said. "Now that we know his secrets."

"Oh that rat thing was bad," the woman said with a laugh. "By the way, the marshal is coming later to ask you about the attack on you."

"He's worried about your being attacked."

The soup smelled mouthwatering. He was convinced he was in for the best of care. But the slightest movement reminded him how pain-racked he really was. The talking in his delirium bothered him. If his babbling had made no more sense than what they had mentioned, his secret about the gold was safe.

Mary Jo proved the attentive one. She fed him and read the Phoenix paper for entertainment. He enjoyed the lilt of her voice.

"Gold Town," she began. "Woman shoots man in saloon."

"Read it to me," he said, puzzled but anxious to hear the story.

"An incident in a local saloon left one man dead and the grand jury sent a verdict of innocent for the woman who shot him. Oleta Brown, an employee of the Golden Palace Saloon, was declared innocent by reason of self-defense. The deceased John Doe, reportedly under the influence of spirits, entered the establishment firing a pistol, which inflicted damage of over two hundred dollars to the fixtures. The deceased repeatedly beat the night watchman over the head with his pistol when it was said the public servant tried to arrest him. Miss Brown at this point shot him with a forty-caliber derringer. The unidentified John Doe was assigned a plot in the local cemetery. The verdict of the grand jury was welcomed by local citizens as fair and serving justice. The watchman Ed Martin is recovering nicely and should soon be back on duty."

Numbed by the laudanum Doc Branigan had prescribed, Whit stared at Mary Jo. He tried to compare her to all the other women in his life. But his thoughts began to ramble and then he remembered the baby in the orphanage. He promised himself he must soon go see about the child.

Two pain-filled weeks later, he finally was able to sit up for periods of time in a chair. He had become accustomed to Mary Jo's attention throughout the day. He grew to hate it when she had to leave with the Judge or the handyman that brought the rig around for her. The gentle reassurance of her soft hand squeezing his made her presence seem so important.

When he apologized for not being able to hug her, she merely smiled and assured him they would have plenty of time.

"Are you really going to go to the job sites tomorrow?" she asked.

"If you will drive me?"

"I think you are rushing this," she warned him, then kissed him on the forehead and prepared to leave.

"I must go now. Jose is waiting."

Whit's impatience did not speed his recovery. Mary Jo drove him about in the light buggy. The gentle sorrel mare responded to every command. For his own precaution, he carried the small Smith and Wesson .22 in his jumper pocket.

They were coming down the hill when he saw Williams lounging against the wall. He could hardly doubt the man's involvement in the beating as he read the cold look on the man's face. If the lawman had planned the beating, how he must feel that his plan had reversed on him. In their passing, Whit did not misread the harshness in Williams's eyes. Though he had not broached the subject, he wondered if the chief marshal had ever considered his own employee responsible for the attack.

When they got beck to the house she gently took his arm.

"I'm going to have to stop imposing on you," he said.

"Why?"

"Because," he said in a half whisper as they slipped out the front door. "There are things in my life still that would shock you. I don't want you hurt."

"What things?"

"I need to get a baby boy away from an orphanage."

"A what?" she asked quietly.

"See I told you it would never work," he insisted.

"No, where is this wife and baby?"

He covered her mouth with the tips of his finger. Upset with her outburst, he looked around to be sure they were alone.

"I don't have a wife, never have had one."

"Where is the baby?" she quietly persisted.

"In an orphanage in Phoenix."

"When will you go get it?"

"You aren't upset?" he asked with a frown.

"No. I can go get it for you."

"No, this is my job to handle as soon as I'm well."

He drew a deep breath that made his head flash with pain. He bent over and kissed her. He did not want to leave her as he went to the waiting rig. His secret was out about the child. He pulled himself up beside Jose. He could see her waving from the porch. The revelation had not upset her

Whit gradually improved. In the following days, he missed Mary Jo's company. His legs made long strides from job to job. His side felt practically healed, as the days of spring grew longer and hotter.

He caught up with the teamster Gil McQueen unloading in Marcus' warehouse.

"They tell me you've been pretty sore?" Gil asked.

"A little," he admitted, helping carry in a keg of nails.

"Did you make enemies around here?" the teamster asked.

"Do you have any?" Whit asked anxious to dismiss the man's questions.

"Say, I got a special interest in your welfare. If you need a couple of big fists and hard toed boots, this Scotsmen will come at a moment's notice."

"Who ever did it will slip up," he said. "They do, I'll be ready for 'em."

"Hey, I know some guys around Wickenburg can learn a lot," the teamster offered.

"If you do learn anything," Whit asked. "Let me handle it?"

"Sure. But you're good for business and I kinda take pride in helping you get started here."

Whit chewed on his lower lip. The time had come to trust someone. McQueen was his best chance. "I need a favor?"

"What is it, man?"

"An old prospector that got killed left me a map to a mine in the Peraltas before he died. I want to take a week off work and go look for it. He has an old burro that smells Apaches. I want you to take it to Phoenix for me, then fix me up with couple more donkeys and some pack gear. Can you arrange it secret like?"

Gil frowned. "Why secret?"

"Old Clay was killed for what he knew," Whit said softly. "I had to have someone to trust."

"I'll handle it. There won't be anyone know where you're going."

"I'll pay you," Whit said.

"When I get it all handled," McQueen said, unconcerned.

"In two weeks, I'll be coming to Phoenix," Whit said, anxious to at least spend a few days looking for the gold.

"Where is this burro at?" the teamster asked.

"Liggett's livery."

McQueen raised his voice. "My nephew will be proud of that burro."

Whit realized that Marcus was close enough to hear them.

While the small man crossed the yard, the teamster gave Whit a private nod of confidence.

A week later, Whit was seated on the boarding house porch with his landlady. He had just returned from dinner at the Barnes house

"Are you promised?" Missus Rathford asked as she stood at the porch rail.   Whit looked up from cleaning Clay's .44/40 Winchester.

"I guess so," he said quietly, concentrating on the rifle that he had fired two dozen times in 'broken bottle' canyon. Accurate enough for the model, he decided. The rust was reduced to scaled places on the barrel and receiver under his patient oiling. Whit shook his head the weapon had lacked a lot of care in the past.

"Are you listening or am I talking to a cigar store Indian?" she asked.

"I'm sorry," Whit said setting the rifle across his lap.

"Do you two plan a wedding soon?"

"I still have a few things to iron out," Whit said.

"She's a very sensible young lady," Missus Radford reminded him.

"Oh yes, that teamster, McQueen, came by today. Said his nephew liked the burro just fine and it worked out good. Now you don't have to pay that tobacco spitting Mister Legget for its care."

"Thanks," Whit said. That was word that Gil had everything set in Phoenix. Tomorrow, he would speak to Marcus about sending him to Phoenix to buy hardwood flooring. The man had mentioned such a need, Whit trusted his boss, but the less Marcus knew of his plans the better. Mary Jo only knew of his search for the child. Whit drew a deep breath, the whole trip to the Peralta's might be a fool's errand.

He had allowed Mary Jo to read the note from Sister Mary Kevin in reply to Whit's letter of inquiry. The reply was vague but the sister did confirm a boy by the name of Whitney Brown was residing at the home. Age, nine months—that fit. Whit felt the name was no coincidence; he imagined Oleta's sarcastic laughter as she gave the child his name.

"Will you build her a new house first?"she asked?

Whit realized his mentor was still asking him questions.

"Probably a shack," he jested.

"I doubt that," Missus Radford said with a shake of her head.

He had two goals before he made firm wedding plans. One was to find the child and the second to go to the Peraltas and look for Cordova's treasure. Mary Jo had said she couldn't wait to help him with the boy. What if she became upset when he brought the boy back? No matter, the memories of his own years in the orphanage were enough. The boy no matter what would have to come out of that place.

"What ever is bothering you tonight has you quiet as an Indian," Missus Radford said.

"I'm sorry. I just have a lot on my mind," Whit apologized. "Like who will do what while I'm in Phoenix."

"I will leave you alone," she finally said.

Whit thanked her.

In the night, the cicadas were creaking, Whit mused how the Apaches should be gone from the Peraltas to the cool high country. This would be the best time to slip into those mountains. Though it would be hot and dry, he had a better chance to miss the red men.

The night before leaving, Whit hardly slept. He rose in disgust and disassembled Clay's .44/40 before fitting it into the case he had purchased for the trip. Whit felt guilty about leaving. Marcus had assured him that Bob and Frank could keep things going for the few days that he would be gone. The Jewish lumberyard man had been kind to him; he hated to leave just as Marcus had a burst of new business. Perhaps he would have to come back and work. What if the gold was only the figment of that Mexican's prison tormented mind? If he found enough gold bars? All the money in the world. What would that be like?

As he fretted, Whit compared Oleta again with the straight-backed Mary Jo. One so fiery that the recollections made him shudder. He pictured Mary Jo again as she stood on the polished hardwood, concerned yet stiff even as he had kissed her goodbye.

Sobering, he picked up the carpetbag. The small .22 was in his side pocket. It was still dark outside as he headed downtown. The early morning stage would leave for Phoenix before dawn. If someone followed him, so be it. He would find some way to shake his elusive enemy.

Whit remained across the street in the shadows while the hustlers hitched the horses by the lamplight. Marcus had purchased the ticket for him the day before. Whit planned to move at the last moment. The bag in his hand already felt sweaty in his grip.

He listened intently. Footsteps approached from the darkened street behind him. His right hand slipped in his coat pocket and gripped the .22. His back set against the adobe wall he stood ready, his tender ribs a grim reminder of the past altercation. This time, he resolved, it would be different. Greatly so.

"Whit?" His heart stopped. It was Mary Jo.

He released the pistol as he peered out in the darkness, concerned for her safety. "What are you doing here?"

"I'm fine, Daddy brought me. I had to see you off. Her hug warmed him as he shook his head.

"You be careful," she said, looking up into his face. He kissed her quickly for the stage was about to leave.

"Get back to your father," he said and headed across the street.

"Wait!" Whit shouted to the driver. He tossed the bag up to the shotgun guard, he turned and saw the Judge drive around to get his daughter. He climbed in the coach, feeling relieved that she had someone to care for her.

Too anxious to be tired, his excitement prevented him from even considering sleeping. There were dim outlines of low mountains, shadowy giant cactus that appeared as monsters. The spiny cholla glistened in the weak starlight. A mixture of pungent greasewood, bitter dust, and the horse's lather filled his nose as he rocked with the stage.

Time to change horses. Whit climbed down in the pre-dawn light to stretch his legs. The horse handlers were busy out in front changing teams. In the doorway, the tall driver, an aloft man was sipping down a cup of coffee while the guard spoke with a Mexican woman. Whit watched the driver toss the rest of his cup away. He seemed anxious. "All aboard," the man said and headed for the coach. The coach was underway in the growing light of dawn.

Phoenix. Whit was confronted by a sleepy green oasis wedged between small mountains as he climbed out of the coach in the oppressive heat of the afternoon.

"*Senor* Ralston?" a small Mexican boy called as Whit caught his bag from the guard.

"Yes," he said, smiling at the anxious youth. "*Senor* Mac sends me to take you to his place," the out of breath youngster said as he wrestled the bag from Whit.

"What is your name?"

"Peppe," the boy announced.

Whit noticed a man in high top boots leaning against

the wall of the stage office. He was idly whittling and seemed more than casually interested in Whit's arrival. Whit touched the hard revolver in the suit coat's side pocket then hurried after Peppe.

Mounted on the buckboard, Whit glanced back at the man with his pants tucked in his boots. Who was he? No casual loafer. Whit settled back in the spring seat as the boy skillfully drove the fresh team through the congested traffic.

At the freighter's wagon yard, they found Gil McQueen seated in an unpainted captain's chair with his back to the door. He turned slowly and nodded at Whit.

"Well, Peppe got you," the teamster winked at the proud teenager.

"Yes, he's a good boy. How is everything else?"

"You're all set up. I sent your burro to Mesa. It and two more will be packed and waiting. My friend Sanchez says they're good animals and there will be plenty of supplies for a week. That will cost you thirty dollars. A little expensive, but Sanchez is not one to talk. "

"Fine I need to go visit the orphanage of Saint Peter's before it gets too late."

"Peppe can do that," the teamster said leaning over to spit in a brass spittoon. "I guess I can ask you a thousand questions. But if it ain't illegal, I'll take your word about secrets."

"It's not illegal," Whit assured him.

"Peppe bring him to Margo's at supper time," McQueen said and then missed hitting the spittoon. He waved off Whit's offer of money. "I'll get mine later."

For a long moment, Whit studied the church with the towering adobe bell towers and the ornate carved wooden doors. Finally, he climbed down and went to the side door. Whit removed his hat and knocked on the door. His heart felt heavy as he waited. What if the boy was gone? Adopted.

"Yes?" the nun in the black habit asked.

"May I see Sister Kevin?" his voice a little constricted.

"This is a bad time," the sister said anxiously.

"I've come a long ways. Tell her Whit Ralston is here from Wickenburg. I'm sure she will see me."

"Come inside," the nun said and closed the door before leaving him. He could hear the voices of children. They sounded happy. He never remembered ever being happy in the days he spent at such a place.

Another nun came down the hall, older than the first.

"Mister Ralston?"

"Yes, sister," Whit said.

"I am Sister Mary Kevin. If you will follow me I will show you the baby that you wrote of."

He nodded and moved after her. Entering a side room, he heard a child squall. Several babies were crawling on an Indian rug with two sisters seated amongst them.

"This is the Brown boy," Sister Kevin said, lifting

"Sister, can I leave money for his care . . . . until I can make a place for him?"

"Yes," she waited for him to continue.

"Do you want to hold child up for you to see him?" Whit felt a lump in his throat. The child had Oleta's blue eyes and its facial features looked familiar.

He gave the child back to her. Whit nodded that he had seen enough, he stepped back.

"Do you plan to marry his mother?"

Whit grimaced at her question. There was no way to lie to a woman of the church. "That's a very personal matter, Sister Kevin. I'm going to leave forty dollars for his care. If I don't return in a month then consider me dead."

"Dead?" She frowned at him. "I don't understand?"

"I have business to attend to. If in a month. . . ."

"I understand," she said, accepting his two gold double eagles. "This is generous of you. We shall pray for your safe return."

"Thank you," Whit said and left still feeling remorseful and promising himself they would be kind to the child until he could come back for him.

"Did you go to confession?" Peppe asked as Whit rejoined him.

"Sort of," Whit said, glancing back at the church. "Let's go find that Margo's place."

"She has good food," the youth said and clucked to the horses.

Whit noticed nothing out of place in the plaza. He settled on the spring seat and considered the sister's words, 'We will pray for your safe return.'

TWELVE

GIL WOKE WHIT up from his light sleep. Whit blinked against the glare of the candleholder's orange light.

"Get up. Sanchez is here and ready to go," Gil boomed.

"Yeah," Whit said, swinging his legs over the side of the cot and grinding his sleep sore eyes. He had not slept fitfully at all. Either the rats or the creak of the warehouse had kept waking him. He realized there was someone with McQueen.

"Come on," Gil said. "I've got some food and the coffee is nearly done."

"Whit Ralston." He managed to say in introduction with a hoarse voice to the gray bearded Mexican man holding his sombrero before him.

"Sanchez," the man said with a smile as they shook hands. "*Senor* Gil said you wanted to leave Phoenix before the sun comes up."

"You did well," Whit said while he tucked in his shirt. The man appeared to be ill at ease as if he expected that his part of awakening Whit might have perturbed him.

"*Senor*, do you have much to carry today?" Sanchez asked.

"No," Whit said. "Just a rifle and some clothes."

"I will put them on the horse while you eat and have your coffee."

"The rifle and that bag," Whit pointed.

"You better drink a couple cups of this," Gil said handing him the tin mug. "I brought some beans wrapped in tortillas. Figured you'd get hungry before the day was out."

Whit sipped on his coffee and listened to McQueen. "Sanchez is a good man. "His horses don't look like much but they're stout. He'll have you to those burros and on your way. Plus he can keep a secret."

"I owe you a lot," Whit said.

"Just remember," the teamster said. "When you come back from this wild goose chase, get your butt back up there to Wickenburg where the real world is."

"I think you are probably right," Whit sheepishly agreed between bites of the spicy burrito.

Whit checked the cinch and noted that his carpet bag was hooked on the tattered large horn and his rifle was in the boot. It was obvious the horse was small; he held his head downcast. Mounting, Whit shifted in the saddle and wondered if the animal would collapse.

"Whip some life in him," Sanchez said as he swung his own horse around.

Whit applied the long reins to the horse's rump.

It responded in a tail tucking burst to catch up with Sanchez as they rode out the gate and onto the brick surface of Washington Street. Unshod hooves clumped on the pavement under the constant persuasion of reins and the heels of their riders.

By sunup, the two riders were headed east through the salt cedars along the sandy water course of the Salt River. Under the sparse jutting butte, they avoided the farming community of Tempe. At mid day, they jogged eastward on a dusty farm road through the irrigated fields of ripening small grain, grapes and citrus. Both mounts seemed weary, but Whit decided they could hold the bone jarring trot endlessly if so persuaded by their riders.

After topping a steep grade onto a mesa, they pounded over a plank bridge that spanned a large irrigation ditch. Sanchez reined up his horse and pointed to a row of cottonwoods. Whit nodded in silence, relieved the tedious ride was going to have a respite. When Whit dismounted, the horse gave several long snorts of relief.

"I must apologize," Sanchez said with a shake of his head. "These horses are not mine. I rented them from a Maricopa Indian. He promised me good horses. I would hate to see his bad ones."

Both men laughed freely as Sanchez passed his canteen over to Whit. As the water cooled his mouth and the moment gave him a chance to think, Whit wondered if his mission was fool hardy. The mountains were vast, his information sketchy. He mounted when Sanchez indicated it was time to ride on.

Past noon, they rode the spent Indian ponies at a walk up the adobe house lined street of Mesa's barrio. Brown skinned children paused to stare at them. Cur dogs barked with uncertain ferocity at their passing. Spanish voices chattered in Whit's ear and Sanchez acknowledged some of them.

His man signaled a halt. In a stable yard made of tamarack poles bound to gnarled crooked mesquite posts, Whit saw the sleepy burros. Before he dismounted, he recognized Jughead. A host of half naked Latin children rushed to take their horses. A matronly woman with a wide girth came to the open doorway of the house. Her face was expressionless.

"Paco!" Sanchez shouted, searching around with a frown of impatience. In answer to his call, a older man under a shapeless hat and wearing a poncho emerged from the brush arbor shed.

"*Senor?*" the man apologized to Sanchez.

In a burst of Spanish and a black scowl, Sanchez gave the man several instructions on what he should be doing. Whit loosened the cinch on his saddle before the youngsters towed the horse away.

"Come," Sanchez said. "We will have food."

At the house, his host stopped to introduce him to his wife. "This is *Senor* Ralston, Mia Theresa." Then he indicated a chair for Whit at the oak table. Whit listened as the man ordered food in Spanish. Theresa went off to get it.

"You wish to leave?" Sanchez asked with a wry glance around.

"Yes. Can I get past the farms by dark going east?" Whit asked.

"Oh, yes," Sanchez assured him.

He dipped his beans up with a tortilla and washing them down with raw red wine. He regretted the lack of flatware but the spicy food tasted good. Half way through, he acknowledged the meal to the man's wife who was posted in the kitchen door, Whit surmised she waited for further demands.

"I followed the list that McQueen ordered," Sanchez said. "Plenty of *frijoles*, corn meal, dried peppers, jerky, salt, lemons and dried apples, sugar, enough for a month. Two water kegs and a hundred rounds of .44/40 ammunition and ten boxes of .22 shells."

"Sounds like all I'll need," Whit said as they left the house.

Whit stepped in to help the old man finish loading the last two burros with a toothless grateful grin from Paco the two completed the chore.

Sanchez smoked a corn shuck cigarillo, his back to a corral post. The wide sombrero shaded his face from the afternoon sun. Whit felt the man's eyes follow him as he loaded shells in the Winchester and then stabbed it into the saddle scabbard. Sanchez frowned when Whit swept off his Philadelphia hat and pushed it at Paco.

"Tell him I want to trade," Whit said.

Though the older man swept off his old sombrero, he hesitated to take Whit's hat. But Whit insisted and installed the bigger sombrero on his own head. Then he drew the small pistol from his coat pocket and struck it in his waist band. stripping off his coat he indicated he wanted Paco's poncho.

The old man's eyes widened in great disbelief.

Sanchez said something in Spanish. In hasty awkwardness, Paco removed the garment and exchanged it for Whit's coat.

"Now I see a Mexican," Sanchez exclaimed at his discovery.

"If they ask you, tell them I rode north," Whit said.

"Si, *norte*," Sanchez said to Paco, who seemed confused.

Whit paid the old man two silver dollars that he pressed in his unwashed palm. "*Gracias.*" Then he turned and handed Sanchez a ten dollar gold piece.

"No, *senor*. McQueen has paid me."

"To buy yourself better horses." Whit adjusted the chin strap of the hat. Paco came back from the shed bearing a worn pair of leather leggings. Whit could not understand his toothless babble.

"He wants you to have them," Sanchez said. "To protect you from the cactus."

Whit accepted them graciously and put them on. They weren't the style of chaps he had worn as a cowboy and barely came below his knees, but he realized they would help ward off the spiny plants.

"*Via Con Dios!*" Sanchez waved as Whit swung up in the saddle and prepared to depart. Under the floppy hat, he rode out of Mexican town jerking two pack burros behind, barely drawing a bark from a dog. His small train rumbled along at a snail's pace through the farmland of irrigated citrus, dates, and lucerne.

By sundown, Whit was beyond the agriculture and in the greasewood and saguaro clad desert. He viewed the sunset's blaze on the distant purple face of the Peraltas great face. While a lonesome rooster quail whistled off in the desert, he hobbled and took care of his burros. Far way, a coyote yelped at the night wind.

When he finished watering and feeding the animals from the collapsible canvas buckets, he paused and considered the day. Jughead was more comfortable to ride than an Indian pony. Clay must have known that. The other two burros were amicable, but hardly with a personality like horses that he had owned. Whit wrapped himself in a blanket on the ground and tried to dismiss all his misgivings about this search.

At dawn he mixed parched corn meal and brown sugar in a cup with water and ate it by the morning starlight. The glowing sunrise haloed the distant mountain wall as he methodically loaded his animals. There was no hurry, his goal was at hand.

"Long eared *compadres*," he said aloud to the sleepy burros. "The riches of Cordova are just past those heights."

THIRTEEN

WHIT SPENT THE first day scouting the face of the mountain, careful to avoid Gold Town and the main road. In late afternoon, he found a bitter spring tank. Carefully he checked around the pool of water, but there were only some unshod burro tracks, deer and other game prints around the edge. With the .44/40 across his lap he squatted down and appraised the mountain. This looked like a place to make his first camp before he assaulted the range.

The camp site appeared secure enough. He licked his dried lips and listened as a top knot quail called off in the greasewood. The he considered a cup of coffee for his parched thirst. Again he turned his ear to the quail's whistle, Clay had said the Apaches used the bird's call to signal one and another when they crept up on unsuspecting enemies. Pursing his mouth, Whit practiced the bird's whistle. He smiled as the burro brayed in protest. With a sigh, he rose to go unpack them. He decided to try a small fire. Any smoke might carry to a sensitive copper nose. There would always be a risk of detection. He just hoped as he unloaded his panniers that the red man was gone to the higher mountains for the summer.

The animals were hobbled and free to graze. Whit took the rifle and decided in the few hours of daylight remaining to search the wall for an entrance. He followed the game trails to the talus rockslide base, then picked the most used path and started upward. Deer hooves had scuffed past the spiny cholla, the jumping cactus with a thousand needles ready to stick the nearest man or animal. He climbed higher and higher until he was satisfied the way would led him into the mountains.

His heart pumped as he mounted more of the steep pathway; he paused before starting in a deep chasm cut in the face and searched the top of the sheer walls above him. It was wide enough for his pack animals. He pressed on until he gained the summit where the fresh wind swept his sweaty face. Breathing deeply, he leaned on his rifle and viewed the interior of the Peraltas.

Awed by all the mesas, canyons, and mountains, he stood soberly considering his mission. Blind canyons, steep hostile cactus studded slopes, dry water courses--he realized there were a thousand places to search. Far to the north, he knew there lay the unseen river. Perhaps twenty miles to the east, from what he could recall of the man's hoarse voice in the cell to where Ratero emerged to escape the Apaches. Standing up straight, Whit strained against his sore muscles. If the man had not lied, he would find the ruins that held the gold.

Whit hurried back to his camp. There was no sign of another soul. For the time being, he had more things to worry about than Indians. He must refill the water kegs with the bitter spring water. Without any knowledge of another source, he needed to be cautious and use the chalky tasting water.

At camp, he built a small fire to cook some beans and chilies which he ate as the sun set. Then he sipped on the luxury of strong hot coffee as the topknot quails slipped out of the brush and went to water at the small pool. Other families joined the first brave ones; soon they ignored him and the burros.

Starlight and a quarter moon silhouetted the burros' long ears as he coaxed them with feed bags of corn meal. While they ate, Whit saddled and packed them. At last complete, he shoved the Winchester in the saddle boot and mounted his riding burro. His eyes were on the mountain washed in the pink first light. Three days and he would come out. By then if he had no promise of locating the ruins, he would go back. Marcus was counting on him and Mary Jo ... yes, he owed her his allegiance. He put his heels in Jughead's sides.

"Let's go find that damn Mexican's gold."

Sure footed, Jughead picked his way as if he knew the trail up over the mountain. Whit gave a last look at the desert floor and entered into the narrow canyon followed by his obedient pack animals.

He started at the hoot of a large owl; before he had recognized the call, his hand had sought the .22 pistol in his waist band. Chiding himself for over reacting, he replaced the revolver. But as the summit emerged, Whit was relieved to be out of the chasm.

Nothing seemed out of place as he viewed the jumbled labyrinth beyond. The trail appeared to go off the mountain and disappear in the twist and confines of the canyon country below him. Whit drew a deep breath and booted Jughead on his way. This was the start, he mused, with deep concern. Either way he was committed.

Though out the first day, his pack train followed a little used old trail that he hoped was the Spanish track. Sun warmed the depth of the canyons as Whit examined the steep slopes for signs of a cave. In late afternoon, he paused on a high divide. A strong wind whistled through the greasewood bushes. Whit decided to make camp among the house size boulders. After he fed and watered his burros, he found a comfortable spot to seat himself with a view of the trail and he settled down to gnaw on hard jerky, washing it down with bitter water. Nearby the picketed burros shuffled in search of a comfortable place to stand and sleep. Tomorrow, he promised himself, he would find something that Cordova had spoke of. He tried to suppress his concern that the Peralta's might never have used the trail he had taken. No, he promised himself, this was the way.

Noon, the second day on the move, Whit grew impatient with Jughead. For no obvious reason to him, the saddle animal started acting up, snorting and shying like there were unseen ghosts.

"Damnit!" he swore aloud. Jughead laid his ears back in anger as if he would refuse to continue. Whit raised his hand to smack the balking donkey on the head.

Something clattered on the rocks. Whit heard the next arrow whistle through the air. The rear donkey brayed in pain. Twisting in the saddle, Whit tore out his pistol. Three howling archers were poised on the large boulders just above him. When he fired the .22 at them, he realized they were mere boys in their teens.

But the shower of arrows from their bows convinced him they were Apaches to reckon with. The pistol's dull pop made them wide eyed. One was hit. Whit fought with Jughead as his enemies withdrew from his view to aid their fallen comrade. The wounded pack animal was kicking and braying in pain. All Whit could see were two arrows bristling in its pack.

"Damn," he swore to himself. His heels pounded Jughead's ribs as he sought to depart. The burros seemed equally anxious and they scrambled up the steep trail with Whit unlimbering his .44/40 as he rode. There was no sign of pursuit, but he wanted to take no chances. There was not even a hint of where the three arrow smiths had gone.

On top of the mountain, rifle ready in his right hand, using his free arm, he extracted a small game hunting arrow from the burro's rump and settled her down. The wound was not deep, which eased his concerns. Carefully Whit scanned the vast mountains. If there were young hunters about, then tribesmen would be in the mountains. Why hadn't the damn Apaches gone to the high country, he wondered, almost sick with the knowledge they had not left.

"Jughead," he said aloud to the burro. "Next time, you need to give me better warning." Whit shoved the rifle in the scabbard and swung his leg over as he re-mounted. Settled in the saddle, he began to breath easier, regretting as they crossed the long mesa that he couldn't stop and let the animals graze the thick stand of gramma grass.

Whit reined up on the far side of the plateau and searched behind. There was no sign of his enemies and the burro acted calm. Relying on that assurance, he headed off into the next canyon. Nothing seemed out of place.

When he gave Jughead his head, the burro found a side canyon where sweet water seeped into a rock basin. Whit, however, frowned upset at the signs that he found of the presence of javelinas. At boot top high, dried dirt marked the sidewalls from the mire they had wallowed out below the tank. Whit was anxious to give the cranky javelinas a wide berth and after watering his animals swept his own tracks from the area.

He selected another blind canyon nearby to store his pack goods high in the rocks so the wild pigs could not root them. While he worked, Whit considered the boys who had attacked him. Just bushy headed youths wearing red bandanna headbands, armed with small game hunting arrows. Whit visualized the Apaches, dressed in white cotton breech cloths and knee high boots. But their screams or war cries he recalled as blood curdling sounds.

He regretted wounding the one, but salved his conscience with the notion that the three of them would have probably killed him if they had the chance.

That evening, Whit huddled in his blanket as the cool night air settled in. Cordova never said this would be easy. What did he say? Twice he had returned. Whit picked at his memory. The Apaches had scared his tough companions away. A grown buck would have shot a steel tipped arrow capable of killing that burro. Or even himself, Whit realized. They would not have used the tiny stone point intended for a cottontail or packrat.

How many Apaches were in the Peraltas? Why weren't they up on the pine clad Mongollon Rim?

Licking his cracked lips, he listened to his burros shuffling. In the morning, he would find them a place to graze while he searched on foot. A pack train was too vulnerable from an attack. With his hand he drew the blanket closer over his shoulder as a wolf's chilling howl cut the night. Cordova never said it would be easy, he reminded himself.

Whit knew his legs were strong enough to carry him. All the hiking around Wickenburg from job sites had hardened him. The Apache was no enemy to take lightly, nor were they foolish. He would need to be more careful to survive. Whit thought again of the boy warriors as he fell asleep.

Day three. After turning the burros loose on a grassy mountaintop with some potholes of water nearby, Whit worked his way along the tops of bluff. He took stops to view the country and check for any movement in the canyons.

Satisfied there were no Apache's in the canyon where his goods were stashed, Whit returned to the side canyon to refill his canteen with the sweet water. He entered the narrow sided cut, apprehensive about the javelinas.

But they had come and gone, rooting in the soft mud below the spring's overflow. At least, Whit though they didn't bathe in the spring itself. Then his eye caught a glint of dull yellow in the muddy wallow. The javelinas had unearthed something.

"My gawd!" Whit exclaimed as he squatted down to see. "It's a gold bar." Treasure of kings. The monetary symbol of civilization. With his quaking hands he removed the heavy bar, his whole body shook with the excitement. His eyes burned on the bar until salty tears ran freely down his cheeks. His fingers brushed away the mud and he saw the P-brand encrusted with dark mud.

Shaken by his good fortune he washed the bar off with spring water. How had it gotten there? Had one of the mules, separated during the fight, carried the treasure there? Part of the men had been split away. Were there more bars in the mud hole? Whit's heart stopped. He would go get the small pick and shovel. Damn, he sighed, what luck--javelinas and an attack by Apaches--still his whole world had been changed by the discovery.

Whit hid the gold ingot inside a water barrel cached with his supplies and then he cautiously went back to dig up the ground around the spring.

Nothing. Darkness found him exhausted, the area unearthed but no more gold. He restored as much of the digging as he could and took a deep drink at the spring. How much did the bar weigh? Thirty-five pounds? In darkness, he plodded back to the other canyon where his packs were stored, still uncertain of the weight. But he retrieved the ingot from the tepid depths of the water barrel and hefted it in his hands for a long time while coyotes heralded the rising moon.

"Here I am a rich man and can't even risk fixing a cup of coffee," he said aloud so he would hear his own voice. The words made him feel as if he had companionship. As he sat with the gold in his lap, and ate hard jerky while he mused about all the time that had elapsed since Florence and the long day in the saloon. Whit gave a shudder. The find was too good to be true.

Dawn came and Whit ate cold cornmeal and brown sugar mush with a lemon that Sanchez had packed. He put the gold bar back in the barrel and took his rifle. His intention was to climb the high cliff above him and have a vantage point to view the land. He needed to mark the place in his mind for his return. Without help and more guns, to remain much longer in the Apache's presence seemed foolhardy.

Cautiously he climbed up the narrow chimney until he topped out on the mountain's narrow backbone. Sprawled on his belly, he observed the mountain where he had left the burros, the far peaks beyond the Salt River. To the south, Whit could see the desert floor, hardly a few hours walk. That was the direction that Peraltas men wanted to escape. But the Apaches had driven Peralta's men north. Mexico lay in the opposite direction, Whit surmised, still feeling very elated by his find.

Mean as it seemed, he felt grateful for the Apaches-- they had scattered the Spaniards allowing him to find the bar. And those young bucks attacking him forced him in the right direction.

Whit paused as the small herd of black javelinas scurried around below him, on their way to the spring to wallow and drink. Live and let live he said, giving a small salute to the wild pigs. Whit removed his wide brimmed hat. After the pigs left he would go down, refill his canteen, and head south on foot. To stay much longer would only reduce his chances to survive.

The eternal wind of the mountain tops picked up.

His ears detected a new sound. It was the metal clicking of shod horse. A voice carried, "Ho."

Someone was coming from the same direction he had taken to reach the mountains.

Then he saw the riders, barely larger than match sticks, dwarfed by the giant saguaros. White men, they wore hats. Scooting back, with his knife, he cut some tough creosote brushes for camouflage. Carrying them back, he lay on his belly and listened. His heart was pounding as he watched them descend single file off the mountain.

The two in the lead were civilized Indians; they wore hats but rode different than the white men. Whit silently swore as he recognized Williams, the deputy from Wickenburg. The bare reddish haired arms had to belong to the Captain Stevens of the guards at Yuma.

The contingent disappeared behind the lacy chaparral and rocks as they wound their way down the slope. Six armed men, Whit decided. Two were Indian guides who were looking for sign as they rode in the lead. Damn. The Organization had found his trail.

Face down on the rock ledge, Whit tried to control his breathing. He considered the rifle beside his hand. He could kill or wound several of them. No, he might never get out of the mountains alive doing that.

He raised up to peer through the branches of the strong smelling bush. There was a boy with them. No, he saw it was no boy. Oleta rode with them. Damn her, there was no one he could trust.

Then their voices carried clear on the wind.

"How many burros?" the Captain demanded. "Three huh?" Whit recognized the voice from the prison. Wallace was with them.

"Do the Papagos figure that we're close to him?"

"They ain't blood hounds," the Captain answered. Whit's heart stopped. One of the scouts had headed for the spring canyon. They would find signs of him and tracks around to his stashed things and the gold. His fingernails dug in his palms.

"Come on," the Captain shouted. "He says there ain't nothing but javelinas in there."

Collapsed on his face, Whit began to breath again. The damn pigs had covered his tracks and saved his treasure.

"Where did the son of bitch go?" William's voice carried.

"We'd probably all ready have Cordova's treasure if you hadn't beat on him."

"Go to hell," Williams mumbled.

Whit heard the admission, but Oleta's laughter knifed him. He felt empty over her part in the conspiracy. A working girl yes, but a spy for The Organization. . . Whit shook his head.

Before dark, they would discover his burros and begin back tracking for him. Whit swore under his breath, he would need to leave the mountains with the one bar. At least he knew by the man's own admission why he had been beaten. That matter he intended to settle himself.

A buzzard drifted over as they rode on out of earshot. Whit comforted himself that so far he was not a meal for the bird of carrion.

A flicker of movement on the mountain made him focus on the trail, from where they had descended. Was it a deer? Whit first saw the bandage, the three young Apache were scouting The Organization's back trail. So, Whit mused as he studied them, he had not killed the one. Busy place, first the prison conspiracy, second the Apache trackers.

They looked like children at play as they checked the animal prints on the trail. They fired a barrage of arrows at a tall-eared jackrabbit. The hare hesitated on a knoll and the hunters hurried for another shot. Then they searched about for their arrows. In knee boots and loincloths, the miniature warriors were just boys growing up.

Returning to the trail, Whit watched them examine a fresh pile of horse droppings on the path. After inspection, they seemed in agreement about the obvious fresh spore. Then, half-crouched like mountain lions, they went on down the mountain.

In a little while they seemed to tire of the game and went back over the mountain from whence they came. Out of view, Whit finally allowed himself a sip from the canteen. After dark would be the time for him to move on. By starlight, Whit picked his way off the mountain top. He knew the military road skirted south of the Peraltas. That would be a good way to get back to Wickenburg.

FOURTEEN

"TALL HORSE IS here," a yard boy announced.

"He's an Indian," Gil explained. Then he laughed. "Wait till you see him."

Whit stepped outside and saw the tallest Indian he had ever seen. Riding a powerful roman nosed gray horse, the man appeared to be a giant. He led a dark roan with a log chain for a lead.

"Tall Horse," Gil shouted and headed to greet the new arrival.

"You need a little help, wagon man?" A broad grin spread across his copper face like a prairie fire.

"I need a lot, that's why I sent for you." Gil motioned for one of the yard boys to take his horses. "Tall Horse Johnson, I want you to meet Whit Ralston."

Exchanging formalities, Gil and Whit explained the project as the big man nodded his understanding from beneath the flat brimmed unshaped hat.

"Chato is there," Tall Horse grunted

"Chato?' Whit remembered the name of the chief from a newspaper story. "Why is he still there and not up in the pines and mountains?"

"No place to go. The Army has him cut off. They are patrolling the river to the north," Tall Horse said in his halting accent.

"All I saw were some little boys," Whit said. "They shot at me with little hunting arrows."

Nodding, the Indian agreed. "Days of the bronco Apache are few."

"What tribe are you?"

With a flash of his stained teeth, Tall Horse grinned. "Apache."

"And I'm vouching for him," Gil said, encircling Whit's shoulder with his arm. "General Crook himself gave that big buck a letter that says he can go anywhere he wants. Seems old Tall Horse saved his life about ten years ago."

"I never doubted it," Whit said. "Is your lady friend Margo feeding all of us tonight?"

"She sure is and you're buying." Gil laughed. "We're all working for you."

Whit slowly shook his head. He had an army, now he must feed them. As they gathered to walk the few blocks to the cafe, there were more than the usual number of folks loafing around on Washington Street in front of the stables. Where was The Organization? There had been no a sign of them. But they were around. He wondered if he could keep the lid on this whole operation much longer without starting a public gold rush. Perhaps Chato's presence in the Peraltas was staving off a stampede.

They saddled by starlight. Whit took a lot of pride in the activity at McQueen's wagon yard. The quality of the stock impressed him as packsaddles forked stout mule's backs and the force Gil had promised him materialized. His army was on the move. Soon it would disperse in three directions to confuse the curious. Whit knew livestock, but he realized with his outfit packed and ready that Gil had obtained the best.

Yett saluted him as he rode past and out the front gate with the long line of mules under their diamond hitch canvas loads. Their hooves clattered on the brick pavement, breaking the morning silence. Tillman, standing in the stirrups, rode by at the rear.

Whit nodded his approval and headed for the Kid, who held their horses. He swung up in the saddle as Gil came beside his stirrup and spoke in a soft voice. "Florence Junction, we'll all be there Saturday night. "

"Thanks." He motioned for Wylie to lead the way out of the yard. Two days' ride ahead. Whit marveled at the ease of the bald faced horse's gait. There was no comparison to Sanchez's Indian pony. He almost laughed aloud.

They rode in silence up the darkened street.

Yett's pack train was already out of earshot. Whit marveled at the swift disappearance of his team. When they struck the sandy road that paralleled the Salt River, the Kid spoke up. "You figure the Apaches will attack us?"

"They might. But a gang of white men might be a bigger problem."

"Who are they?"

He turned and checked their back trail before he settled in the saddle. "Some men that have been after me since they figured I learned about this gold."

"Hard cases?"

"Prison guards. Yes, they're tough and will stop at nothing. They killed an old man I worked for just so he wouldn't warn me. Beat to death an old prospector who taught me about surviving in those mountains. They probably even killed the man who told me about the mine—Cordova."

"Was he a friend?"

"No," Whit said, while exhaling deeply. "Cordova never had a friend. He poured lye in that old man Pasqual's eyes years ago so he couldn't go back and find the gold."

"Damn," the Kid swore. "You keep tough company."

"The same kind of thing I preach to you," Whit said booting his horse into a lope. "Crime damn sure don't pay."

"You've got the gold," the Kid shouted as they raced.

"It hasn't been easy and I don't have all of it yet." He would have traded a normal life of cow punching and horse breaking for those lost years. And maybe even for the gold.

That night, Whit and the Kid camped outside of Gold Town. Whit lounged around filled with anxiety. He wanted to learn if Oleta had returned to her saloon haunts but also feared any word might tip off The Organization of his plans. He sat with the blanket over his shoulder, too anxious to sleep. He listened to the yap of the coyotes and watched the half moon rise over the towering black wall of the Peraltas. Was this a fool's mission? He closed his eyes and tried to think of his plans.

In the morning, they skirted the mountain face. Their horses were fresh and Whit was anxious to reach Florence. Halfway around the great rising island that the Peraltas's range formed, he cut the tracks of the pack train.

"That Yett is ahead of us," he shouted at the Kid.

"He was old General Crook's best Packer in the sixty-nine campaign."

"Who told you?" Whit asked amused at Wylie's knowledge.

"They all worked for him. Tillman, Yett, McQueen, and Tall Horse—that was how General Crook got them Apaches on the reservation in the first place."

He sawed Baldy to a walk. The Kid rode back, his horse breathing as hard as Whit's mount and both blowing hard.

"Guess I picked a hell of an army?" Whit asked.

"You sure did."

The mules were picketed on a line. They had been brushed and their orange and brown to black coats shone in the afternoon sun. Nearby the packs were stacked in an orderly fashion and Yett was building a fire when he looked up at Whit and Wylie's approach. Tillman squatted with a rifle in the crook of his arm on the far side of camp. They were professionals.

"Coffee be boiling in fifteen minutes," Yett promised.

"Any trouble?" Whit asked the man as Wylie took their horses away.

"Had to shoot one mule. He must have got on loco weed sometime in his past. Before we crossed the Salt River, he had a big fit. Nothing else we could do. That never shows up in an animal until you get them in a sweat. We brought the goods though."

"You moved right along."

Yett looked up, a broad smile spread across his face. "Tillman and me didn't want to miss nothing. Did you see McQueen?"

"No. Why? He's not due here till tomorrow."

Yett laughed as he stuck more limbs on his growing fire under the granite coffee pot. "Tillman and I wondered if he ain't got too round-butted sitting on that wagon seat to fork a horse this far."

Shaking his head with amusement, he stood and studied the plaster walls of the stage stop in the distance. "Anyone been down there?"

"Tillman went, told them we were taking army supplies."

"Anyone suspicious-looking hanging around down there?"

"He never mentioned it. He's pretty hawkeyed. If he'd thought we had trouble, he'd said so," Yett said. "Hope you like rabbit stew."

"Is that going to be supper?"

"Yeah, and ain't one of them we shot today over five years old."

McQueen and Tall Horse arrived at sundown. Wylie and Whit were savoring the stew and Dutch oven biscuits. Tillman had taken his plate and gone up on the rise to look out. Whit had noted the man's ways and intended to speak to him to show his appreciation.

"Where do we go from here?" Gil asked, taking a place near them.

"I went in north of here and wandered around. We need to find a mountain east of where the Spaniards could hold off the Apaches and where they could do smelting. That was Peralta's headquarters."

"Tall Horse, do you know of such a mountain?" Gil asked.

"A day's ride," the Indian said without looking up.

"You know this mountain?" Whit asked.

Tall Horse raised his head and looked him in the eye. "Two big rocks to grind ore a long time ago."

"That's them." Whit's heart pounded. "Is there a canyon north of there with a cliff dwelling in a cave on the wall?"

The affirmative bob of the un-creased hat in the growing darkness forced Whit to close his eyes. Thank God.

"Who else besides the damn Apaches are between us and that place?" Gil asked between bites.

"Oh." Whit drew a deep breath. "Just some prison guards, a couple of Papago trackers, and a dance hall woman. "

"I want to know about this woman." Gil said.

"Guess we've all been fools once in our lives," Whit said, grateful for the growing darkness as his face warmed.

The pre-dawn air had a chill as they saddled and packed. Yett's coffee had opened Whit's eyes from the first hard sleep in weeks. He felt secure with these men, much better than he had felt alone.

Coolness was the ingredient that made the mules hump. Tall Horse held the wilder ones under his arm like they were lambs, while Yett swiftly packed the animal. No effort, Whit mused, amazed at their skill and timing. They weren't ordinary packers, he sighed as he mounted Baldy, they were the best.

"Do you figure Tall Horse knows this country that well?" Whit asked, sidling his horse close.

McQueen grinned. "Don't ask him for the names of those bucks out there with Chato, unless you want to know them too."

"What does that big Indian do for a living?"

"He catches wild horses. He saved old George B's butt and Tall Horse ain't talking about that either."

Whit settled in the saddle. The Indian had taken the lead, Yett behind him as they headed north through greasewood taller than a rider. Whit remembered this part of his return journey to locate the military road.

During a pause for a break in a broad, dry wash, he rode up to Yett. There was no sign of the Indian.

"Where's Tall Horse?"

"Scouting. He's being sure we don't ride in on Chato. Old Gil ain't fell off his horse has he?"

"You ain't no kid yourself," Gil said as they laughed at his expense.

A horse was coming. Men's hands went to their gun butts. Tillman cocked his Winchester. Tall Horse appeared.

"We rest horses, then run for mountain. Plenty sign where the Apaches been." The Indian shook his head as if he was filled with doubt.

Whit booted Baldy in close.

"Are the grind stones still up there?"

"In a pile of cactus," Tall Horse said.

Reassured, Whit thanked him and dropped his reins.

Why did he doubt everything? They still had to reach the mountain alive.

Mentally, Whit went over Pasqual's story. The old man's had been the same as Cordova's tale. The gold that they had not lost during the attack was with the captain's corpse. Whit refused some jerky that Yett offered. Tall Horse knew the canyon. Why were they sitting there?

"Can we ride, Tall Horse?" Whit asked.

The big Indian nodded.

"Everyone get ready," Yett said. "If one of my mules goes down, let's save it."

"Yes, I hope we need all of them," Whit said. "And watch out for each other, too."

Tall Horse turned his big half Percheron gray around and shouted at it. In two jumps, the powerful horse was halfway up wall of the gulch. Yett followed and Tillman went up another path that paralleled the mules' file.

Gil rode in the middle. The Kid and Whit kept the rear going as they raced toward the mountains through the chaparral. Pistols in hand, they crossed the wide flats and drove up a long exposed backbone of the foothills. Pressed in by the live oak on a flat, they rested their horses for a breather. Silent, each man warily searched for any sign of an enemy on the towering sandstone face of the mountain to their north or the desert they had just crossed. Mules snorted and Baldy shook, rattling the stirrups on Whit's boots.

Canteens quenched their thirst with tepid water while a lone topknott quail called from the spiny scrub live oak.

Whit saw Tall Horse was ready. No words were necessary. They began the ascent up the steep mountain. A mule lost his footing and the Kid was quickly off his horse and beside it. He pulled the wild-eyed animal to its feet and it rejoined the others. Whit brought his saddle horse to him. There seemed no time for words.

The hair on Whit's neck stood on end. A crawling sensation churned his stomach, and he expected that any moment a feathered arrow or shot would reach them. The trail became so steep their horses were forced to cat hop.

Horses screamed in protest and their cries mixed with the strain of mule's squeals as leather groaned and hooves fought for hard ground in an avalanche of broken rock. Then Whit looked up and saw the mules disappear from his view over the rim. They were near a flat, he reasoned, as Baldy charged at the heels of the Kid's bay.

A final burst and they were on the top of the mesa.

A cool wind swept his face as he raised his hat and wiped his sweaty brow on his sleeve. They had made it. He looked up and saw the scrubby jack pines. This must be Cordova's mountain.

"Anyone see anything?" McQueen asked, walking in circles to work out the stiffness.

"I sure felt they were there," Whit said, loosening his cinch. "What about you Tillman?"

The man stopped and set the butt of his rifle down between his boots.

"I've been in worse places, but by God then they were shooting at me. I'll go out on the point and keep an eye out."

"Thanks," Whit said, knowing the man was going to stand watch on the trail they had just maneuvered. "We'll all take our turns at guarding."

Tillman was noncommittal as Whit watched him squat down. Whit went on to speak to Tall Horse about the canyon and the cave.

"This place where the ancient ones lived? How close is it?" he asked.

"Half a day's ride." Tall Horse was saddling his spare horse.

"Can we get there safely?"

"I will see," the big man said, reaching under for his girth and drawing it up.

"Don't take any chances. We can all go if necessary."

Tall Horse only nodded and mounted up. He headed the gray horse to the north and Whit watched him ride down into one of the side canyons that fed from the mesa top.

"Where's our scout going?" Gil asked, joining him.

"To check on something. He's pretty close mouthed."

"He's up to something. But I'd stake my life on him."

"We have."

They went back to Yett's new campsite.

Whit listened to Gil's plan for guard duty.

The Kid took the first shift and prepared to replace Tillman.

Having filled the new oiled rifle full of shells, he paused. "I'd kind of like to just see something to shoot at."

Yett looked up hard at him. "You may get all of that you want with Chato before we get out of here."

"You think he's that bad?"

Yett just nodded and busied himself with his cooking.

Whit loaded another new rifle across his lap. The packer was no coward, but the man seemed to have a deep respect for this Apache chief. He checked the sun. They had made record time getting there, still nearly half a day of daylight left. But they would have to wait on the Indian to return. Whit set the loaded gun aside. If he hadn't felt so anxious he would nap.

Whit took his turn of guard duty on the mountain's edge. The wind in the jack pines played an eternal song. Gil brought him coffee as the sun died in a blaze of glory beyond the front range.

"I promised these men big bonuses if we struck gold," Gil said, looking in his own cup. "I should have told you about that."

"If we get it, I'll pay them well. I've sat here for two hours wondering if we ain't in the wrong mountains and I just don't know."

"You think we're close to it?"

"I'm judging what Tall Horse says. The cliff dwelling is close. If that's Cordova's and someone hasn't found it, there is a fortune waiting."

"Good enough for me," Gil said. "I think I hear the Injun' coming in. Let's go talk to him."

Whit hurried back to the campfire. Tall Horse squatted as Yett dipped him out a clay bowl of *frijoles*.

"Any luck?" Whit asked,

"Plenty sign. Apaches, white men in the canyon."

"How long ago?" Whit asked. He mentally panicked. The Organization had found the cave and took the gold and was gone.

"I did not go far down. The tracks were a few days old." Tall Horse considered his beans and glared at Yett. "No tortillas?"

"Use a spoon," Yett said firmly. "Like a white man."

"Oh." Tall Horse turned to Whit. "We will go to the place of the ancient ones in the morning."

Whit rose and thanked him. He listened as Yett and the Indian goodheartedly argued about spoons and tortillas. Under normal circumstances he would have enjoyed their bantering. Had the others found Cordova's gold? So close and yet so unsure, he mused, while unfurling his bedroll. He would pretend to sleep. His dry eyes stared at the red-glowing mesquite logs in the fire. Sunup would be a lifetime away.

FIFTEEN

DAWN MUST HAVE been delayed, Whit decided as he lay awake on his blankets. Mules grunted, even brayed in the silent night while one angrily cow kicked at the next one. Impatient with their tethers to the picket line, they and the saddle stock shuffled. Whit sat up, supported by his hands behind himself and closed his eyes. He envisioned Mary Jo coming down the long stairs in her white wedding gown.

"Are you okay?" Yett asked as he stirred his fire up.

"Sure," Whit said with a smile and blinked his gritty eyes. "Just thinking what I was going to do when this is over. You got plans?"

"I kinda wondered if you'd sell us this pack outfit? Tillman and me would like to buy it," Yett said as his fire flared. "Might not have all the money, but I figure we could pay for them and guide some rich men hunting."

"We'll work it out," Whit said, pulling on his boots. "Whose turn is it to guard?"

"I'll wake the Kid, Till's out there now. But he never gets sleepy." Yett rose and went to shake the form on the ground beyond the fire.

Whit went off to relieve himself. Where was Tall Horse? There was no sign of the Indian in camp. The steady updraft from the side canyon cooled his stubbled face. Somewhere down there in the dark abyss was the home of the ancient ones where the Peraltas left their bullion.

Whit turned on his heels. He refused to even speculate on The Organization having found it. Before the day was over, he would either be rich or a carpenter.

"Re-heated," Yett said, pushing a tin cup of coffee in Whit's hand.

"Anyone seen Tall Horse?" McQueen asked as he joined them, buttoning his shirt.

"Good question," Whit said, blowing on the vapors from the hot coffee.

"Apaches hate the night. It must be important or he wouldn't be out there," Gil said.

"He's coming," Yett announced as he crouched by the fire and worked his Dutch oven.

Whit almost argued with the man before he saw the form of Tall Horse materialize from the jack pines.

"What is happening?" Gil asked

"Plenty." Tall Horse shook his head. "The US Army is close by. Greater danger to be run over by Chato's bunch on the run from them than for the Apaches to ambush us."

"Any sign of the white men?" Whit asked.

Tall Horse shook his head. "All old signs, two days, maybe more."

"All we need to do is get to those ruins for a few hours. The treasure is either there or it has already been taken out by others," Whit said, pacing back and forth. "Tall Man can we get in and out quickly?"

"We can try."

"Why would Chato use that canyon?" "

"A wounded wolf runs away."

Whit nodded. He understood the desperation of the hunted. "We better leave two to guard the horses. Yett and I can take a mule apiece. Gil and Tall Horse can be on the lookout."

"Two mules?" Tall Horse asked.

"Yes, if we have any treasure to haul out it will take two of them," Whit said as the big man rose to his feet. "What's wrong?"

"Tie blankets strips on their feet, not make big sound," Tall Horse said and Gil followed to help him.

Whit finished his coffee and let Yett refill it.

"The Kid and I will take care of things here," Tillman said. "It would take a big tribe coming up that mountain to overcome the two of us."

"Thanks," Whit said, watching the gray flare of dawn. He wished it would hurry.

They ate a breakfast of fried bacon, Dutch oven biscuits, and molasses. Whit took the Kid a plate and explained their plans. When he returned, the light was strong enough for Tall Horse to draw a map in the dust with a stick.

"Big cliffs, me on top." Tall Horse explained. "I can see if Apaches come."

"You'll be up there in case," Whit deciphered. "What is the signal if there is trouble ahead of us?"

"From up there." Tall Horse's raucous crow call amazed Whit. It was indistinguishable from the bird's. The men shared a smile.

"Do we have all we need?"

"Couple of shovels, pick, some bags, and canteens?"

"They're loaded," Gil said, handing Whit one of the new Winchesters.

"You guys don't even need me," Whit said goodheartedly, trying to keep the anxiety from making him too excited.

"This is your army," Gil said as they headed for the mules.

"I'll bet you guys didn't treat Crook a damn bit better," Whit said, taking a lead rope for a mule.

"No, we didn't." Gil laughed.

Whit jumped back as Yett's mule reared and tried to buck him off. The packer dug his heels in and the big Indian joined him on the lead. They quickly quelled the animal.

"He don't like his new walking shoes," Gil said, starting off as if nothing serious had happened.

"I swear these were the calmest ones we ever had," Yett said, watching the mule out of the corner of his eye as he followed Gil. Whit fell in behind with his animal, convinced his didn't like the blanket boots either though he wasn't quite ready to have a fit.

Descending off the mesa, Whit could see the chasm through the brushy juniper on the slope. The earth yawned open and the trail twisted around house-size rocks as spring pools spilled over into their path.

He made his mule go slow, less he lose his footing on the mossy places and fall. Farther down the water disappeared in the sand and the narrow trail was dry and dusty.

Looking up, he caught a glimpse of Tall Horse, high on the yellow bluff to his right. Reminded of the young bucks' attack, he was grateful for the man's presence as they wound their way down the narrow route into the canyon. Ahead, Yett's soft cursing of his mule made him grateful his own had settled down. The blankets worked, for there were no sharp echoes in the confines of their world.

The trail twisted around more giant rocks in the very bed of the canyon. In places the canyon floor was drifted sand, and others gravel. The sun shone on the west wall, but the air was still cool on his skin. Willows, salt cedar, and occasional stunted white bark sycamore with flash flood debris piled at its base forced them to detour around.

Whit nodded when Gil pointed with his rifle at the intersecting side canyon. They would be close to the place. Searching the rim of the high cliff, he saw no sign of Tall Horse. That would be as far as he could go, but there had been no crow call.

"Watch that rock face," Yett shouted to him.

Whit nodded and started down the steep polished rock slope. He watched his mule pick his way slowly, then slide the last two feet to the pocket of sand.

"Smell that?" Gil asked, signaling for them to stop. Rifle ready, the teamster proceeded cautiously ahead.

The sweet copper smell of something dead caused Yett and Whit to exchange puzzled looks as they waited with their mules to see what Gil found ahead.

Buzzards rose, flapping their wings as the two men hurriedly tied their mules to some bushes.

"They're dead," Gil called back as Whit came with his rifle ready.

Whit stopped in his tracks at the sight of the massacre. He knew a lot in just a moment.

"Damn!" Yett swore as he joined them. "Who are they?"

"Captain of the Yuma Prison Guards," Whit said as he studied the bloated naked body with the red hair and now faded freckles. His body bristled with arrows. Whit looked down with bile rising in his throat at the corpse of the stigma of his life—Deputy Williams. Either the buzzards or the Apaches had gouged out the deputy's eyes. Whit turned away. The man was also disemboweled.

In anger, Whit fired his pistol at two buzzards feeding on another body down the wash. The ugly birds flapped reluctantly at his raging screams.

Tears welled in Whit's eyes. Where was Oleta?

He found no sign of her. The crude mass burial required two hours in the side of the watercourse. The three men were exhausted, wet with perspiration.

"How much farther?" Gil asked.

Whit shook his head. "Can't be much farther."

He picked up his rifle and started down the wide sandy flat between the two sheer walls. What had the Indians done with her?

He stopped and looked at the towering, wind eroded side of the canyon. Blinking his eyes, he tried to raise some saliva in his dry mouth. There, thirty or forty feet above him, was the cave home of the ancient ones. He could see the adobe walls and the small logs that supported roofs.

"Forgive me Cordova," he mumbled to himself. "I've found it."

"Where?" Gil asked, coming on the run.

"There!" He pointed, fascinated by the view of the *casa* for the ancient ones. No longer able to hold his excitement, he broke and ran. "Bring those shovels," he said over his shoulder.

He scrambled over the centuries-old accumulation of talus rock at the base and pulled himself up by the handholds chiseled out by the Ancient Ones. His breath knifed his lungs and his muscles seemed too weak to perform the feats he demanded. Belly over the adobe rock front wall, he rose to his feet. He viewed the crude stone rooms and juniper stick-waddle ceilings, and the small corncobs littering the floor.

He rounded the corner and saw the spilled, destroyed walls.

"This is where they buried *El Capitan*," he said aloud to reassure himself.

"Whit?" Yett asked. "Is this it?"

Shaken by his discovery, Whit came out and sat down heavily on the wall. "I doubted that old Mexican killer a hundred nights and a thousand more when I got out. We've got a lot of shoveling to do but it looks just like he and Pasqual said it would."

"I hope this beats burying those dead men," Yett said, pulling up his kerchief.

The dust was choking even with the masks as they shoveled away the debris. A thousand years without moisture, Whit decided, as they fought back the rocks and mortar back.

"Wait," Yett said. He knelt down to examine something. "It's a man's hand.

Whit pulled down his kerchief. "They buried their captain here with the gold. I'd say he's right over it. "

They both struggled to pull the half uncovered mummified body back.

"Oh my God!" Whit motioned. "Peralta's gold!"

He could see bar after bar that had been under the Captain's care for so long. He dropped the dead man's arm and picked up two dust-floured bars. Out by the wall, he polished one on the leg of his pants and when he held it out, the sunshine struck it and glinted dully.

"What in hell have you got?" Gil asked from his post across the wash.

"Get over here you crazy teamster. We just struck pay dirt."

"Did you find it?"

"Hell, yes." His words echoed in the canyon. Thirty-one bars were handed down and placed in the panniers on the two mules. Yett cut the blanket rags off their feet.

"Let Chato hear them," he said.

"Be better than one of them slipping and breaking a damn leg."

"Don't mention him," Whit said. He looked distastefully in the direction of the fresh graves. "Even dogs like those didn't deserve to die like that."

"I'm ready to get the Hell out of here," Gil said.

"We have the gold," Whit said, looking back for a last time at where they had re-interned the captain.

Gil waved a rifle at the high cliff when they came in the open space where he expected Tall Horse could see them. Whit saw no movement and cradled his rifle, looking anxiously back over his shoulder, then turned back and trudged after Yett and the two mules.

The long torturous climb began. Mules and men rested every few yards. Gil gave a shout that started Whit and caused him to cock his .44/40, but the mules blocked his vision.

"Just Tall Horse," Yett said. "He's looking around to be sure we were all right."

"Tell that ugly big Injun' that we're all rich!"

Whit shouted, frowning with impatience at the pace of the mule ahead of him.

"The Kid's come down too," Gil shouted back.

"I hope someone's watching our camp," Whit said, still forced by the narrow way to stare at the mule's tail.

At camp the men all came in and feasted on brown beans the Kid had scorched.

Yett made new coffee and they were all contently eating in a circle.

"Fellows," Whit began. "All we lack is a run for Florence Junction. We found thirty-one bars of Peraltas's gold today. Each man will get a half a bar for his share."

There was silence as the men elbowed each other. Then they quietly thanked him.

Whit frowned. "Did Gil promise you more than that?"

"No!" came the chorus and they all laughed.

Whit knew he had pleased them. "Choose sides for guard duty. You can wake me for mine." He put his plate in the boiling kettle on the fire and went to find his blankets. He was the sleepiest rich man he knew.

No one woke him for his shift, he decided, as he swept his blankets back. His eyes were sore from sleeping so hard. Yett was clanking the lid on his Dutch oven and barely looked up as Whit went off to relieve himself.

He returned and dropped beside the squatted Tall Horse.

"Is there any sign of Chato?" Whit asked, accepting the cup of coffee from Yett.

"No sign."

"Can we make a run for it?"

"I think so," Tall Horse said.

Whit rose with his cup. Time to get out. Time to leave this cactus land of Apache arrows. Mary Jo get on that white dress, I'm coming with Whitney and all the gold. We'll be riding a bald face sorrel horse.

The mules were finally loaded, Yett poured water on his fire. Whit held the lead rope to one of the gold-bearing pack mules. Gil had the other. If they lost any of the other mules, they were to go on. The two mules bearing the gold had to be protected and gotten out. They had gone over the plan several times. Still, he was anxious to be on the military road, and to have the last race over.

"Whit!" the Kid shouted. "It's the Army and they've got prisoners."

Whit handed the lead for his gold mule to Tillman and swung into the saddle. The horse circled several times until Whit brought him to a halt so he could study the procession coming down the canyon below.

A yellow guidon fluttered as the blue uniforms formed a guard around a line of several ragged captives. Whit sent Baldy off the edge, down the trail. The horse's hind legs sledded as Whit leaned back. Saddle leather creaked as it strained. Baldy went down the mountain. Sure-footed, the mountain horse found places to slow his descent and then leapt down for another.

The Army had noticed his perilous flight and had stopped to watch a crazy man come off a mountain at breakneck speed. Three-fourths of the way down, he reined the hard-breathing horse up. Even the dark eyes of the Apache prisoners followed him. Whit spurred the horse on.

An officer with a non-com rode out to meet him.

"Whit Ralston," he said offering his hand to the officer.

"Lieutenant Gage," the man said. "You made quite a ride. Can we help you?"

"I just wondered if you had captured Chato."

"That's him," Gage said, pointing to a small Indian on horseback wearing Williams's hat. The Stetson was too big but Whit did not miss the mischief in the Apache's eyes.

"Well, Whit, did you find the damn gold?" a woman asked as she rode her Indian pony up close to him.

"Pardon?" Whit asked frowning. He didn't know her.

She wore a trooper's coat. Her face was dirt-streaked and her hair matted with dried grass. But her blue eyes told him it was Oleta.

"Yes," he said softly and nodded as the lieutenant prepared to move on. He turned in the saddle to view his pack outfit coming off the mountain more sensibly than he had. Tall Horse came on his big gray, then Yett and the two mules bearing the gold, next Tillman and the rest of the pack mules, then Gil and the Kid waved their hats from the rear.

"You owe me part of it," she screamed behind him.

Whit turned and shook his head. "No, not now, Oleta. You better go with them."

He reined Baldy around and set the sorrel horse in a gallop to rejoin his crew and the gold as they filed off the mountain.

THE END

DUSTY RICHARDS GREW up riding horses and watching his western heroes on the big screen. He even wrote book reports for his classmates, making up westerns since English teachers didn't read that kind of book. But his mother didn't want him to be a cowboy, so he went to college, then worked for Tyson Foods and auctioned cattle when he wasn't an anchor on television.

But his lifelong dream was to write the novels he loved. He sat on the stoop of Zane Grey's cabin and promised that he'd get published. And in 1992, his first book, *Noble's Way*, hit the shelves. Since then, he's had 153 more come out.

If he can steal some time, he also likes to fish for trout on the White River.

Facebook: westernauthordustyrichards
www.dustyrichardslegacy.com

DUSTY RICHARDS

"He is a Natural Born Storyteller!" —Brett Cogburn

PRESENTS

THE
BRANDIRON
SERIES

Harrowing Tales of Life and Love in the Old West!

A BRIDE FOR GIL

THE MUSTANGER AND THE LADY

THE TEXAS BADGE

THE CHEROKEE STRIP

GOLD IN THE SUN

CPSIA information can be obtained
at www.ICGtesting.com
Printed in the USA
LVOW10s0000170117
521187LV00001B/2/P